# FATE OF THE UNKNOWN

# FATE OF THE UNKNOWN

## Shedrick B. Seton

*Village Tales Publishing, Minneapolis, MN*

A catalog record for this book is available from the Library of Congress:
Library of Congress Control Number: 2024901529
ISBN-13: 9781959580034
eISBN: 9781959580041

Published By:
Village Tales Publishing
Minneapolis, MN 55429
www.villagetalescreatives.com
www.villagetalespublishing.com

Layout and Cover Design by: OASS


Printed in the United States of America

# *Dedication*

To Hawa Yolian, Roseline Korleh, Wilisa Bulls, and Comfort Whitfield, my imperfections and errors never stopped you from believing in me. I appreciate you. Thank you!

To those mothers (Oldmas) who knew me from nowhere but would put aside a little bowl of food for me (when I was in school), Thank you!

To my parents, Joseph Zarazoegar, aka (Zara) Seton (Late), and my mother, Kemah Clinton, thank you! Like countless other whose fathers' names were discontinued and handed new names, you cannot question fate, but we who are alive will have to live with the burdens, shame, frustration, and longing this 'generational trauma' left us with. A cross too heavy to bear!

And to the memory of the late Paddy Ilos, Sr. (author of Marry is a License); you saw the direction of this story when helping to edit the first edition of the Candlelight Magazine. I salute you, Sir.

Writing this book is a task worth taking; firstly, for my country and, secondly, for my people. Although I have friends and family on both sides, this evil in our nation's past must be told. Not for fame or favor or to denigrate the black Americans who colonized (with the help of the United States) the land and people but to point out those missteps and where it has landed us. I salute our ancestors (Americo-Liberians, natives, recaptured slaves, those from the Caribbeans, and all those who settled in Liberia for greener pastures, struggling for the upkeep of this land we now call Liberia. I hope this fictional story will open our eyes to the true nature of the land of self-determination and liberty. It's now the land for all blacks, whites, etc., and we must craft laws to protect and promote all, not a selected few.

To Anita, Shanita, Silvia, Sharon, Shedrick, Jr, and Angel, my love.

# Contents

*Ignorance of each other is what has made unity impossible in the past.*

—Malcolm X

# Prologue

## SOMETIME AROUND THE 1300S-1400S B.C.

Long before the Portuguese explorer Prince Henry ex-
plored Africa in the 1400s, looking for routes to the Indies, the
Romans had already visited Africa, establishing outposts in
Sala Colonia and Mogador. But the Normans and the Portuguese who came later, went farther along the continent, interacting with the inhabitants, and started several years of trading history. Their language the inhabitants learned and spoke,
cultures and food adopted and internalized, and places they
named like Cape Palmas, Cape Montserrado, Cape Mount, St.
John, and St. Paul Rivers are still visible today. Other natural
beauties these explorers saw were Fisherman and Piso lakes.
Mano, St. Paul, St. John, and Cavalla rivers formed spiral lines
and curved into the hearts of the evergreen vegetation.

Those who visited the landscape and the people they saw appeared mysterious, unschooled, dark, and uncivilized to the better way of life of the Greeks, Romans, or Christians.

Scattered within the dept of that jungle are people who had their unique way of life, a form of government that was built on patriarchal principles and patrilineal, an uncommon way of doing business, valuing relationships and trust, morals, and a tradition to respect the elders, and being obligated to strangers. Over time, the inhabitants cultivated and made that unknown place their habitat and a haven.

Mystical is a name given to a place that is unknown or a place that is not understood. So was the land after the Lioness Mountains, the Grain or Pepper Coast, the land of the Malagueta pepper, Pigmy Hippo, and Pepper birds, which appeared mystical.

The Grain Coast always appeared spooky to those who saw it the first time. But deep into the mystery is its uniqueness, debunking those who saw other civilizations in the eyes of their own. The pages of history have shown that such persons or people are always colonizing the condemned civilization. I believe instead of condemning and colonizing, one must seek to have an open mind and find a midpoint for the goodness of all but not measure your territory against another and indoctrinate people into believing that your language, way of life, civilizations, cultures are better and pure.

So, as the Grain Coast and other civilizations grew and expanded over the centuries, several curious people (from the mid-world and the new world) with different intentions launched a framework for a new world order. Curious as these people were and lively as they appeared, secrecy (Masons) and lies (equality) were the darkness they embraced. They started by establishing trading posts, and then came the Bible—its spiritual, moral, and ethical principles to soften and bring the inhabitants to submission. The inhabitants learned and spoke the languages of the curious people who came to their land.

Years of trading brought closeness and familiarity, allowing integration and respect for the laws. The curious people cunningly entered all fraternities and even learned the languages of the locals. In return, they admitted some locals into their friendly societies but kept the rest to hold them together and to propagate their ulterior motives.

As Shakespeare said in Macbeth, 'There is no art to find the mind's construction in the face.' As pure as they appeared, those people were as friendly and cunning as they assembled their gallantry and marshaled their troops into action. They turned the tide and began the greatest looting- spree, colonizing, land grasping, civilizing, and subsequent enslavement.

It is believed the quest for supremacy and control over others created opposite options: heaven and hell, life and death, right and left, rich and poor, good and bad, north and south, morally and ethically acceptable and unacceptability into the one-world community. What gives man the quest for the end? It's the options that pump the adrenaline into a man's ego. The ego transforms the meek into God-like beings and elevates them to an unbelievable height. This elevation is a place of comfort, and those who arrived realized that instability would sway one into humility or recklessness, wickedness, and/or conceitedness. Those curious people believe every other civilization beneath their reasoning.

They conceptualized the takeover of the earth; they crafted their ways of elevating themselves as the better minds. Staging a takeover and dominance, learning from all cultures, and collecting their uniqueness while using damnation and every means to their advantage and promising an acceptable path.

They didn't invent anything but borrowed from the greatest minds of others or past civilizations. He rebranded everything, snakingly made them his own, and intentionally refused to give credit to the rest of mankind.

Man is cunning and always sees the end. But he will not reveal the hard roads and corners of the means. To him, the world is an amazing and beautiful place. As someone said, *"Beauty lies in the eyes of the beholder."* The colors constantly displayed attract the sight, capture, and appeal to the psyche. So, what makes the world so beautiful?

Its colors made it breathtaking. Everything, from human to biodiversity designed and colored beautifully. One is not essential without the others.

Despite colors, age-group, appearance, level of comprehension, limitation and desires, mankind strongly believes he is mandated to replicate heaven and its heavenly hosts. God, the supreme and all other hosts are lesser deities. Who has seen heaven? No one, but it is depicted through the Bible.

Therefore, man only has a mental picture based on the narrative from the Bible. This mental picture of heaven travelled through generations, made no mention of pigmentations except assigned roles and responsibilities. No strategy on getting slaves and colonies, no mention of supreme race. Not even black or white. When God took the children of Israel from Egypt (from slavery) as mentioned in the Holy Bible, He promised them a 'Land' of their own but not taking over a land and a group of people. They fought their way to the Promised Land. God placed them among strangers. He wanted the children of Israel to be sociable, considerate, and tolerant. No pigmentation. Are black, white, or colored human adoption?

What is 'black' that I cannot comprehend? Is black evil or inferior? What is subsequently 'white' that I still can't comprehend? Is 'white' good and supreme? But what I see is not 'black' or 'white' but humans. Who made the world color-blind? Falsehood? Fear? Blasphemy?

Lie, a word so powerful as the human mind. Truth, a bleach for cleansing lies. Where there is no truth, the human mind consumes what is fed to it, and it becomes a culture—an acceptable truth. And when the acceptable truth contradicts actions, the people become numb and resist. Therefore, the curious people's plan for Africa started with trades and then the takeover.

With a calculative plan, those curious people began sifting the uniqueness of Africa and reprograming its people through several gruesome manners. Africa now became that abandoned warehouse used to supply instruments, cultivators, provisions, or storage to fuel the material wealth of the system.

The greatness of Africa (the old world) has been highjacked and erased. It positions as the fulcrum for self-actualization, governance and cradle of civilization must be understood and acknowledged it greatness as seen in Egypt, Timbuktu, and other places. The 'curious people' buried Africa uniqueness and refused to acknowledge its greatness. Instead, they spread the falsehood that Africa is dark, deprived, uncivilized, and always in need. Have they forgotten that the entire earth was once dark, deprived uncivilized, and always in need? Was Egypt or Timbuktu dark and in need? Those civilizations grew and advanced because they hosted people from different cultures.

A multicultural environment will always spring into great development. Egypt was successful because of its multicultural policy which spurred inventions and development. Things that were invented were sold to people from other cultures or at the trading posts. Several years after the declined of Egypt, trading posts still displayed the arts learned from Egypt.

These trading outposts in Sala Colonia and Mogador were famous for their dye-making. The local purple dye-making industries, cultures, the gold, and diamond, and the inhabitants-their different kingdoms and structures of governance were proof that the old world had some level of advance cultures and civilization. So, those who wanted valuables searched all over the world. The Portuguese took it further.

The Portuguese or Normans travelled further than the Romans. Taking detailed notes and mapping out lands, rivers, streams, people, cultures, and civilization.

From their Phoenician-styled ship, they specially noted in their travel-book the mystical appearance of the western portion of the land south of Sala Colonia and Mogador.

At first sight, a blanket of mist surrounds and covers the huge vegetations. Within the mist, mushroom-like treetops sporadically positioned, and mountains appeared in the background like sketches. Birds would be seen hovering over the fog.

It was midday, the ocean roars as soapy forms spread over the brownish African coastline. Insects scattered into the air escaping the creeping waters. A school of bird maneuver scattered and ambush in the tree. Targeting the preys jumping as the soapy forms approached.

Some birds sat singing beautifully, apparently full of spoils. Their tweeting mixed with the thundering sounds of violent ocean waves and of different creatures echoed into its quietness, thereby releasing a spine-chill feeling.

But deep into those densely tropical surroundings, people were caught up in their socio-political, cultural and economics ways of life. Those people, seem from the vantage point of the Portuguese, long ago travelled from the north and east and, sought that place as refuge from the constant infighting among kingdoms, unpredictability, religious dominance and harassment, famine, and the search for good vegetations.

Among those who settled beyond the lioness mountains are the Gola, Kissi, Dan, Bassa, Kpelle, Mende, amongst others. At first, survival within that enclave was a matter of life and death—a noble endeavor.

Overtime, understanding, and tolerance prevailed; a purpose for survival drove their differences into mutual defense mechanism. Along the centuries, these agreements were tested and mended, bringing better understanding amongst the various tribes. Thus, fighting in its true essence was reduced to sporting activities that brought pride and dignity to the winning tribes.

Throughout the ages, men had accepted life as a race which begins within the womb and ends at death. From the onset, youthfulness accelerates the epinephrine into childish and foolish ambitions and, in old age, men realize his flaws and raced to replenish the exhausted energy. But that did not stop the gaining and failings. Since then, men realized that every baton had to be passed down to the next generation.

There were many competing activities to test men's strength and endurance and to award those who succeeded. Like humans, the community competed with other communities to prove their superiority. Therefore, men went against other men in the name of the king and kingdom-community.

Members of the community were subjects of the king. They live for him and most time die for him. He made the laws that directed the affairs of his subjects. The land was his; his family was of noble blood. He passed judgement that were executed by the grand masters. He had council of noblemen that sat at his table, running the affairs of his kingdom. All these narratives were deliberately omitted from the history books.

The Grain Coast, for a very long time, was governed by kings. Each tribal kingdom pays homage to a king—their father. That king protected his people from war, diseases, and famine. The kingdom looks up to him as their spiritual father, a man chosen by some kind of deity. Stories were told of kings who performed some mysterious tasks, or led his people to where they live or, were sent by the gods of the great forest. This age-old form of government impacted the people's mental wellbeing. Over time, it became a culture and a normal way of life. They didn't know that another form of government would come in conflict with their way of life which politicians will use as switch to control and use. In the moment, whatever was done, was done in the name of the king. Even if they are competing, it would require the blessing of the king. People pushed themselves further or died for the king or kingdom. All kingdoms chose the best among the bests to represent his kingdom in any noble endeavors.

Those who were chosen to partake in this noble endeavor were known to be ferocious and vicious. A belief that life on earth is a race to the highest point where endurance pays. Obtain not by work but by amulet given through the grace of the gods. They never questioned life, why it placed them into a community, but they fought to their death to defend what they did with life for the good of their community. A believe system that promoted unity and understanding within their kinship. So, they raced to the top for fame and failed in shame.

It was believed those who made it to the top received special charms from their ancestors, blessed, and satisfied by the spirits of the unknown. If someone failed or was defeated, that meant his ancestors had angered the spirits of the unknown and cursed their generation in previous lives. Therefore, they were paying the price. In a patriarch society, like the one in the Grain Coast, the men bore the burden. The boy-child was the superior gem; they head the established structure.

The structure placed men at the head of the family. Several families made a community. The survival of every community was in the wisdom and strength of its people, especially the men. Though limited by cultural rules, women were placed alongside men, operating their own societies guarded by rules crafted by themselves. If any man broke or went into the women's shrines, that man (no matter what) his status would be dealt with according to the rules and regulations laid down by the hierarchy of the women societies. Therefore, women were allowed to compete in battle and sports.

So, like a rivalry among humans in reaching the top, kingdoms (themselves) must prove their standing among their peers. To reach that position of respect and supremacy, friends must turn into enemies; enemies must form alliances with enemies or make new friends and, survival of the strongest unavoidable.

As for the weaklings, as well as the defeated, the matter of subjection and slavery were a way of survival or consolation. People from the losing town, including all collaborating towns, would become slaves to the victor until the town is liberated by what was term as a new tier one noble. Tier one and two, a structure that supported the winner-takes-all concept. Eventually, town and people were moved like a game of chess in the region, later known as the Grain Coast.

The Grain Coast, like the rest of Africa, has stories that are extraordinary to that particular region. To preserve their stories, they told it orally or used graphic illustrations in caves and rocks. The stories of the Green Coast, were told orally and what is written, were heard from the storytellers about the various tribal countries before the founding of the Republic of Liberia.

The storytellers began with the Dan People. The Dans are a group of people who migrated from the north, some said, the Sudanese areas. Gio is only a section of the Dan tribe. The warrior king, Grougbay Zobaneeay, drove out the cave people to secure a pathway for his people to the ocean. He settled his people two hundred and twenty-five miles from the ocean.

Grougbay changed his name to Dan, to portray himself as the true father and spiritual head of the people. The uniqueness of the Dan tradition is the crafting of special masks and children named in order of arrival in the world.

In reality, Dan is a tonal language made of several dialects, residing side by side with the Maah tribe. They made Gayn-Bgar (GB) their traditional food, a food developed to sustain a warrior on the battlefield for several days. GB is made from Manihot esculenta (cassava). The tuber is boiled and pounded and can stay with a warrior for weeks without spoilage. The soup is specially crafted and unique to the Dan people. Its overall exclusivity is the 'GB Medicines'. A soup or source made from dried, pounded okra or special herbs provided a slippery path for the GB to travel down one's throat like a person on a water slide.

The Maahs and Dans have shared cultural life, economics, and power structure. They considered themselves kin and travelling companion. It takes one with good listening skills to know the difference in speech and pronunciation.

The Maah became a protectorate of the Dan Kingdom. And the Gbez Kingdom was added to the Dan Kingdom to cement a pact with King Yanwleh of the Kru Kingdom. The Gbez King Yorkor was captured and killed by Jlakays in the ten-days war.

There are about five chiefdoms of the Dan tribes living in the north-eastern region.

The Dan believes the world is divided into two realms, human and spiritual. The human realm are people and their community and, the spiritual realm are wild animals and spirits living in the forest. The forest is unknown, therefore those who want to venture into the unknown should take on the forms of its habitants.

These generally dark-skinned people are reportedly known for their soaring and temperament. Their region is hilly and mountainous. A Dan would allow his visiting brother to share the night with his wife as tradition called.

King Grougbay Dan urged his people to labor in dignity and conquer all species in the mountains, beyond and, moved into the unknown for powers and glory.

"If you must do something, do it with dignity, unity, and exceptionalism," he told his people. King Dan took on the spirit of mask making, for which he was gifted. His masks, when worn, had special mystical powers that enabled some-one to assume the powers of the unknown. Every elite or se-cret society from the surrounding tribes and kingdoms went to him for their masks. It then became his family and a Dan heritage, and places his family and the Dan Tribe in tier-one noble amongst nobles within the tribal kingdoms.

Down to the south, about twenty-seven miles from the Dan Kingdom are a patrilineal dark-skinned people called the Guerze or Kpelle, situated in the center of the great forest.

This monosyllabic and tonal people travelled from North Sudan around the sixteenth century due to infighting amongst the tribes within the Sudanic empire. It is believed that King Blili Topakwula, molded his people to work hard and become great farmers. His rules extended over the twelve chiefdoms of the Kpelleh country.

'Self-sustainability will keep us alive' became their motto. He ruled his people through several chiefs. The Kpelleh became tier-one kingdom when they won the Kpem-Kpem competition and became the central kingdom for the distribution of crops for a hundred year. Kpem-kpem is a centennial spiritual competition involving all tier-one kingdoms. The winner was allowed to choose any venerable kingdom and people as subjects. Thus, Kokoyah Kingdom was venerable due to the defeat of its protector, the Bassa Kingdom. The Kpelleh made 'palm oil bitter balls' their traditional soup. It's a soup made from Solanum incanum.

Far to the west of the Kpelleh Kingdom is a hoe-agricultural, patrilineal people whose complexion ranges from golden yellow to golden brown. They are the Lorma or Lomagiti, and their father is Failimu Wubo, a Malian prince who in the 14th century denied right to the throne because he was believed to be a son of a slave mother. He led his mother's people down to the south, fighting resistant tribes and established his kingdom at Wubor-mal. The original inhabitants of that region, the Wonos.

The Lormas dislodged the Wonos. The task of keeping his people closer, so that they can feel this power and remain secure was a task he championed. So, he introduced a structuring of his people that reflected an advanced administrative division. Thus, governed his people through series of chiefs who headed autonomous clans, and reigned over the two Lorma countries.

He instructed his people to believe in their culture, and gave rise to cultural institutions like the poro, sende, mornigii, koloi, koitoi, and zarzay. The Lorma held unto 'Torborgee' as their number one soup.

Torborgee soup is made from Solanum incanum plant. Its main delicacy is the oil and the kind of soda used in the preparation of this superior soup. The craft of producing oil and soda to the Lorma. Nowhere on the continent are there people who can produced Torborgee oil and soda, except the Lorma people.

To secure the Lorma People bloodlines, King Wubo, made it a mandate for his people to be friendly, courteous, and generous, but not to absorbed people from different tribal groups or allowed assimilation into the Lorma society.

King Wubo indirectly ruled smaller kingdoms like those of the Bola, Gbandi, and Mandingo people. They wanted security, he provided it. For some reason know to him, he instructed his people to call the Kissi kins, uncles or aunties. Rumors have it that he did it for security reasons, while others said, he and the Kissi king had a friendly bond.

Living closer to the Lorma, is one of the oldest inhabitants of the region (others being the Goa People) are a long-headed, dark-skinned, and slender-limbed people, who possessed advanced cultural patterns and activities, are hardworking, daring, and always made large farms, like the Kissi People or Kingdom.

Legend has it that they travelled from the far east to get to the place called home. Like the Dan and Maah, the Lorma considered the Kissi as kins, the former calling the latter 'uncle or aunt'. Kissi people are known for their bravery and heroism, belligerent and temperamental. They drove out the cave people who lived prior to their arrival.

King Kai Fallah led the Kissi people through the region and established an advanced form of government like the executive, judiciary, and legislature, but founded on exogamous patrilineal clans, with some form of centralized authority. He made it mandatory for inheritance to be passed to the brother, after which it went to the nephew, and built their towns closed to each other, to be able to call for help when attacked by an enemy.

Security of his people within the three Kissi countries was always his greatest thought. Since he had the Lorma to his east, the Limba people in the west, and the Goa to his south, he made sure to maintain friendship with his neighbors. The Kissi made 'Payloo' their number one soup. It is believed that this herbal soup has medicinal properties.

King Fallah secured a treaty with King Golokai of the Goa, Wubo of the Lorma Kingdoms, and those of the Limba people in the west.

All the surrounding kingdoms chose Bella Yalla as the area of peace. Although in the Bella kingdom, the region (Bella Yalla) is believed to be a reservoir of spiritual powers. Bella Yalla is believed to be a secure place for honesty, truth, and security; a self-administering jurisdictional palaver rotunda where nobody could lie or harbor ulterior motives. Being at Bella Yalla was like being checked by higher powers. No one dared to cheat, his soul would be sucked out of his body. And the cheater lifeless body would involuntarily walk to the forest to be eaten by vultures.

Old is old, and one will never know how old age creeps in. Some believe aging travels with the night; erodes the body at dawn. And the older one gets, the fewer are his friends. And the story they tell (as friends) are comedies to young people. Thus, King Fallah and King Golokai had shared values; keeping the histories of their existence from contamination and expressed through their rich cultures.

The Goa or Gola are the second known migrant living south of the Kissi people. They are rich in ancient culture and are noted for their rhythmic and sonorous voices. The Goa people are good dancers and promoters of secret societies, especially the poro and sende. King Bai Golokai led the Goa people to the region and settled at Kongbaa. He reigned over the seven Gola countries.

Closer to the Goa are Prince Duamani N'Kamara's people, the Vai. They are kin to the Mandingo, and are described as proud, intelligent, honest, and peace loving. They arrived from the north around the 15th century and spread into four Vai countries. Like the Mandingo, the Vai will later become followers of the Islamic religion. They developed their own form of writing. Vai and Dei became the protectories of the Goa.

Goa was made a tier-one kingdom because of their position as the great ancient reservoir of tales through songs and dancing. Their gifted ways of singing and dancing serenaded their hosts and had certain spiritual effects. Goa songsters begin his melody with story of their host might, conquest, and powers; dignifying and celebrating their victories over their adversary. As for their love songs, it was borderless. It was the language; the arts that send people into oblivion.

Gao people were experts in singing into people the unending tales of love which brighten the soul or darken it. The Gao people incorporated and accepted Vai people combing 'Palm Oil Soup and Cassava Leaf' (became known as Gbassayama) as their number one soup. The leaves from Manihot esculenta (cassava) were observed and made into soup by the Vai people. They used cassava leaves for medicinal proposes as well as in juju to get rid of an enemy or to 'keep a husband in submission'.

Far away from the Vai and Goa (and beyond the Dey People) are a prognathous, thick-lipped, and dark-skinned Bassa People or the people of the rock. It is believed they established a kingdom along the Nile River in Egypt, and it was known as Abyssinia or Abassinia. Due to infighting amongst the kings, Gbar-sar led his people (on a triple journey) down to the ocean. According to legend, he dragged a hook attached to a chain until it got stuck to where he wanted his people to live. They easily adjusted to their new environment and began living with cave people, the original inhabitants, taking on their cultures and commerce. Their acceptance of shared communities, their Achille's heel.

Three kinds of Bassa came to the shore at the Green Coast: Mamba, Yao-qwah, and Ne-gbem-wlen. Mamba Bassa brought along a highly advance cultures, like making a dead person to wake up, and having the opportunity to walk around relatives, sometimes pointing out the person responsible for his/her death. And a secret society in which members (at a particular occasion) shared their various wives with others, in the name of the 'grand master'. They reside closer to the west near the Dei and Kpelleh. While the Ne-gbem-wlen Bassa went above the Yao-qweah.

As soon as Ba-sor left, King Kai Gbeazon took over as the head of the Bassa people. And all other Bassa pays homage to Gbeazon. The Bassa incorporated 'Dumboy' as their number one food.

Dumboy is the outcome of boiled Manito esculenta tubers. The Bassa people demonstrated their intelligence in developing these tubers into several categories: dumboy the higher stage, 'gritter dumboy second higher, and fufu as the lower form. Fufu is mainly for the sick, and people who wanted it soft. More to this, is what the Bassa people invented to support the swallowing prepress. They invented what is called 'pepper soup' and, its extraordinary medicine, the 'Dudu'. The world prepares soup, but the Bassa people created *Pepper soup*.

At the far east of the Bassa people, are the Klao or Kru people. King Yanwleh was the famous but fierce king along the Klao Coast, whose reigned extended over all the Kru countries. He had eight wives, including a head wife, Yourkor, and a political wife, Mardea (meaning new woman in the Bassa language) who he married as a token of peace with the Bassa Chief, Daywon. His political seats were in Jeaklon, Settra (the superior of all of the Klaos countries) and Nana Kru. He had chiefs in surrounding towns who supported his administration.

Another tribal people called Klaos, were King Yanwleh's People. Like their king, the Klaos were known for their strength and skillfulness in warfare, wrestling, and conquerors of the ocean. He also captured the Grebo and a group of different tribal people, the Krahn, and brought them under his control.

The zealousness, ambitions, and perseverance of the Klao People were absorbed out of the hot or spicy food they ate. They favored Palm Butter, a sauce from pounded palm fruits, which King Yanwleh said it dated back to his forefathers as the source of survival of the Klao people. Palm Butter, a source from the fruits of the Elaeis guineensis tree. The source is spread over boiled cassava.

The tribal kingdoms had their differences, but they had commonality. The issues of security were agreed by all, the production of palm wines was internalized by every country, a form of money was acceptable for transaction, and herbalists were allowed to work across the countries. Authority to lead all the kingdoms rotated amongst tribal countries. This time leadership was in the hands of the Kloas people.

King Yanwleh was the Kloas king. At Bella Yella, he proposed a monetary system to replace the barter system. It was acceptable to all. A mental rod crafted by the best of smiths, fashioned about an inch long to replace the barter system and used by all the countries for transactions of goods and services. Though not portable and without central regulatory, but acceptable for transactions of goods and services. Everyone mutually accepted the rules, no counterfeiting, no price hiking, and no refusal. The penalties were death or expulsion. From the Gola kingdom to the Ivory kingdom and, from the great mountains of the Dan People to the Vai, Bassa and Klao people of the south, people used it for the transaction of goods and services.

Just like King Fallah of the Kissi People, King Yanwleh was concerned about the safety of his people. So, he organized the Jayklay, an army comprised of several thousand men who were trained in several military techniques, including deep ocean swimming and special spiritual trainings, to protect themselves and the kingdom against other tribes.

Twenty Jayklays were in a Bar-tee (an arrangement to create check and balance), and the twenty Bar-tees were five administering commanders. Those five commanders had a place on the king council of elders. The council is comprised of heads of the seven powerful secret societies from all tribal kingdoms. The Leopold, snakes, Bo-yor, Najii, alligator, elephant, the herbal, etc. Settra became a multicultural kingdom, experiencing exponential growth and development and envied by all. He supported making the Sende and Poro societies social and educational, rather than secret. And as a conservatoire that opened to all boys and girls, void of politics. King Nywleh made secret society among his people a matter of choice.

In response to the idea of cooperation, society and the unknown, humanity has been searching for more inclusive ways to live with one another. The Green Coast had several kingdoms comprising of hundreds of cities and towns headed by kings, chiefs and Zoes (caretakers of the unknown) to maintain cohesion. The Zoes laid down rules and presided over cases that were presumed to be above the kings and were tasked to judge between kings and various communities.

Different communities had their own rules and regulations that family within a community must abide by, but the Zoes were the mighty ones. They were men but in the eyes of the community super men, endowed with great powers, and their habitat was out of bound.

Nonmembers, women, and children scurried into their houses when the Zoes would come out for special occasions, like locating witches, celebrating teens who had completed their trainings at the Sende or Poro schools, to judge high profiles cases and on special occasions.

A special team of musicians tasked to play special spiritual songs using mystical instruments were assigned to various Zoes. However, it was forbidden to have the Poro and Sende schools in the same town. The neighboring town or the other town would compete to harbor one of the two. One group of people cut across the kingdoms, the herbalists. Anyone could visit an herbalist anytime, in any kingdom without restriction or fear. Each time an herbalist entered a town or kingdom, he had to notify the chief or the king of his presence.

On the Green Coast during those days, neighbors served as breeding ground for possible suitors for marriage. Marriage within the same town was not common as people mostly considered those within the town limit as relatives. Parents, especially the mother, would go in search of a suitor for her son in the neighboring town. As young as the marked bride would be, the male was responsible to cater for the bride and sometimes for the family until she was of age. Then the groom father would head to the girl's parent home to finalize the discussion—which would involve the two towns. Each group of people within each tribe had a different arrangement for marriage, and the suitor would have to learn and expected to do it correctly. That correctness brought pride and respect to the bride's people, tradition, and her town. However, in every society, there were law breakers, and the pensility awaited him who broke the laws. In a case where the bride was deflowered before marriage, the parents would inquire from the girl the name of the person, if she named him, he would be brought before the town chief to pay damages. The groom (if he agreed) or the girl would be left without a suitor, or the person who committed the damage will be forced to marry her. If it was a married man, he would pay the bride price and she would be added to his wife or list of wives. The woman would be subjected to a rule by the head wife.

The head wife was special. She was tasked with managing her husband's household and coordinating the farming and harvesting of crops and storage. She supervised or apportioned daily or weekly meals for each wife and children. She made sure to maintain harmony amount the wives and the children and judged all disputes. All the children called her Big Ma. Disciplining children was the responsibility of the entire town and each child had to respect the elderly. Big Ma made sure each wife had her turn to perform her conjugal responsibility to their husband. The head wife also played sensitive role in the household, and no other woman will be brought to her husband without her approval. As a matter of fact, she scouts alternative wives for her husband. For example, if she notices her husband had a high sexual craving, she will search the other towns for another woman (younger) for her husband to marry. The wife would then arrange the fiesta and payment.

These marriages were social, but no voided political interference resulted from misunderstanding from trade and commerce. Women and children were given to the other party to avoid fight, and most time these children or women will be added to the king's list of wives and the children will forever become citizen of their hosts. While marriages were organized to quench desires and settle disputes among towns, other towns sought protection from stronger and richer towns. A protectories town will pay a token of appreciation for being protected.

For fear of the Dan people, the Krahn chiefs remained under the Klaos Kingdom. Several Jayklays were stationed within in the Krahn Kingdoms.

Unlike King Khama of the Lorma People, King Yanwleh encouraged his kinsmen to travel and explore other lands and the wide ocean. He forbids indolence and encourages dignity of labor. His greatest motto was 'Prepare them, and they will follow'. So, at an early age, fishing, military, and hunting lessons with specific spirituality were taught to every male child.

Wrestling was the sport to demonstrate readiness to become a Jayklay. A boy will have to wrestle his way to the top. The top ten champions were automatedly enrolled into the greatest team of soldiers.

The Klaos became master of the ocean as fishermen and sea fearers, fishing from their kingdom to the Ivory and Gold Coasts and further down to the Cape of Good Hope while other Klaomen travelled to the north meeting Europeans, and across the Atlantic Ocean to the land of strangeness.

Those who went on such expeditions brought back gifts of different kinds, learned several crafts, got married and brought back their wives and children. As master of the ocean, Klaos had a mental layout of the great Atlantic Ocean. Even before Europeans began to venture into this vast body of water.

Women reigned alongside their husbands and were listed according to seniority—the head wife who ran the affairs of the household, and managed other wives. They secured younger wives for their husband, were responsible for cultivating the land and rearing of the children—instilling moral and ethical disciplines and, allowed their husband to enforce it. Women served as de facto advisers to their husband, and their husband look to them to promote and protect the moral standing of his households.

The inhabitants grouped according to similarity of cultures, linguistics, beliefs, system of government, and social life. Storytellers were there to narrate the events at play. Land was considered superior and never sold. If anyone wanted a place to farm or build a home, his request would be granted by the king or local chiefs. It created friction but communal land principle helped to restore order.

Where there is security, the economy booms and people have surplus that they share with their neighbors and exchanged. As the custodian of all the tribal countries, the Leopold Society had a straight mandate to secure land and waters. Water and land were believed to be a gift from the gods and kept from contamination. Roads to the water were cleared periodically, and all high bush was cut low, twenty feet from town to the forest. Land was distributed and secured through traditional understanding. Trees were planted to show boundaries. Misunderstanding was handled by the *grand master* and the society executed the verdicts. Town and villages were kept cleaned.

The talking Drum was used to send out messages to distant towns. Those with gifts of healing and medications were classified into different categories based on expertise. The bones experts collaborated and shared knowledge with other professionals with special gift. For example, if someone suffered from a broken leg, the bone expert will collaborate with a spiritualist, especially if the person is afraid. He will break a fowl's leg and heal the patient's leg using the fowl. Whatever he does to the fowl, the patient will feel it. Wrestling, diving, canoe racing, and others had champions who contested in the general championships. Musicians and dancers, artists and people from various profession travelled back and forth to various villages without fears of the unknown or intruders.

The Grain Coast was headed by powerful kings and their descendants. They were King Wubo of the Lorma country, King Blili Toakwala (the great-great-great grandfather of Chief Suacoco, a woman king) of the Kpelleh country, and King Gbeahzon of the Bassa country. Also present during that era were King Yanwleh of the Klao, King Bai Golokai, King Kia Fallah of the Kissi country, and King Grougbay Dan of the Dans.

These powerful kings of the traditional countries collaborated to search for and prosecute lawbreakers. It was the period of peace and happiness. A period that is over a hundred years, producing cultures of respect for the elderly, authority, oneness, and opportunities. An era that sought after mutual understanding, obedience, and collaboration for the general good of all. It spurred inventions of weapons of warfare, improve men understanding of the forest and the rivers, animals and fishes, foods, crops, and a commanding importance.

Generations came and went. Communities strived to achieve greatness. The more they competed, the more they exposed their flaws and vulnerabilities. The end results produced grudges and jealousy and intolerance replaced tolerance. The least fortunate competed for the spoils and powers; killing to achieve greatness was the order of the day. Unscrupulous and greedy kings emerged and used the disbanded Jayklay and those of other societies to get at opponents. The threat would come with succeeding generations. And the peace so long enjoyed, like a puff of smoke on a windy day, realized its flimsiness.

## THE GREEN COAST BEFORE 1800S

History is fragile. It can be manipulated or destroyed. But it's imperative that it be preserved and passed on to the succeeding generation. Much is expected of the former in grooming the succeeding while the succeeding is expected to commit his time and learn. So, communities exert every effort in creating the best environment to accomplish this noble task. While the community is preparing for its successor, leaders were doing the same. Kings were expected to choose their successor, and that person would be tutored by an elder of the community through the Poro, Sende or other Societies. During that period, the Klao Kingdom was furbishing. King Yanwleh days were numbered, and he needed his successor.

He chose one among his sons, TappieYou, commonly referred to as 'Gee say fano com' (Leopard has no fear in his Klao dialect). TappieYou will go on to become the great grandfather of the great hunter, Tappie, who established Tappie Town.

TappieYou continued the traditions of his forefathers and made his people stronger that they ruled the Grain Coast for a long time. It was during his reign that the European first reached the Grain Coast.

It is said that when the Europeans first stumbled upon the coast near Nana Klao, due to violent storms caused by bad weather, they were fascinated by the city. The houses were built in a circular but vertical line formation, leaving passage between two adjutant houses. Each house in this vertical line of twenty-seven somehow connected to this large rotunda called the palace. The houses and palace were roofed with palm straws and sticks. The base and walls were plastered with roasted clay. Artists of each household, of different genres, beautified each house and the palace with unimaginable paintings. It was cleaned. The community was not alarm at all. It wasn't the first time for people to stopped by looking for a route to the ivory or gold coast, down the Atlantic. But they were alarmed that people of different skin color could see their home. For centuries, no one from outside had seen Nana Klao. Nana Klao was made invisible in the eyes of outsiders by the powerful sorcerers of the kingdom. What was that age old protection weakened, nobody knew. But King TappieYou called the Zoes to reinstate that protection upon the departure of the Europeans. When the European ship toasted to shore by the angry waves, Jayklays were there to handle the situation.

When the European vessel was drifting into the harbor like a missing child, the Jayklays were in control, but the people were afraid. It was the first time after several years for foreigners of different pigmentation to enter their country.

Within a few seconds, the European ships were encircled by several boats, canoes and swimmers. It is said that Pedro de Sintra raised his hands, the Klao recognized the ship and already questioned, "Why are you here?"

"We are lost," answered the European. "Where exactly are we?"

"In the country of our great king, Yanwleh, peace to his aches!"

"Who is your captain?" one Jayklay asked in the Portuguese language.

"Let him surrender himself to our king, TappieYou," another jayklay added.

The European paused, then said, inaudibly to another European, "How did he know our language?"

The Jayklay watched the movement of hands. It appeared as if the Europeans were having a micro discussion.

"I am the captain," a bearded elderly man, who appeared to be in his late thirty, replied in Portuguese.

While they were still discussing, a team of Jayklays went closer to the ship, tossed a net with hooks and the hooks attached to the edge of the ship. The hooks held onto the dock, spreading below into the boat. The captain and eight crew members crawl into the boat. Later, two Europeans followed with large jars and a bowls. They were escorted to shore to meet the King. A few boats full of Jayklays remain with the European ship.

The European began looking around, frightened, shaking like wet chicken. The Jayklays led them to the room within the rotunda. The entrance was designed in a way that made anyone entering would have to bend over as if bowing to the king. The Europeans bent over and stood erect as they were in the hall. Legend has it that Pedro and his men trembled and were made to knee by a supernatural force when they encountered King TappieYou. The king raised his right hand, asking the strangers to stand.

"Your majesty, I am Pedro de Sintra and these are few of my men," he introduced himself while looking around the hall.

King TappieYou sat on a high stool made of pure gold; had his left hand folded, directly beneath his cheek. The Europeans recognized the gold. He appeared short and chunky, possessing a well-built body. He was dark in complexion, the one-sided half sleeve leopard skin shirt exposed his well-developed triceps and biceps, and the crown made of hawk feathers made him not generally attractive.

Beads of different designs and sizes made from sea-shells were stringed and crossed over his entire body, under his shirt. He also wore beads around his ankles. His pants wrapped around him from back to front like a diaper. But in his kingdom, this was the latest fashion called Gbom-bor.

"I am King TappieYou," an interpreter echoed the king's elaborated bass introduction.

Then the king introduced his cabinet via the interpreter.

"Well, come in peace," he said to the Europeans through the interpreter.

The king broke a kola nut, handed one piece to Pedro de Sintra and said, "We share a piece of our heart with you."

A pretty girl handed to King TappieYou a piece of clay plate containing a brownish powder. King TappieYou dipped the piece of kola nut into the substance, put it into his mouth and chewed it. The plate was passed on to Pedro de Sintra; he dipped the kola nut into the substance and put it in his mouth. As he chewed, his face turned pink from the hotness of the substance. Everyone burst into laughter.

"Once you see a frog coming out of the bush, it is either being pursued by a snake or looking for somewhere to lay its head. What brought you to our shore," "King TappieYou asked the Europeans. His face was without a smile.

"We were sailing down south when we saw this beautiful vegetation and decided to stop and offer our goodwill," the European said, waving his hands at his men.

His men brought out two large jars, a case, and some bowls. The jars were labeled *Brandy* and the case, *Tobacco*.

The European poured some Brandy into a wooden cup, put it to his mouth and tasted it.

"We accept your goodwill and hospitality," he said and handed a cup to King TappieYou.

The king took a mouthful, fringed, and swallowed. Then he nodded his head, appreciating the quality of the liquor.

Pedro de Sintra smiled. King TappieYou ordered his men to bring in four kinjas (bags) full of malagueta pepper, three sacks of liquor (Gba-we-ya-co), two sacks of rice, and six calabashes full of hot pepper.

"This is our gift to you for stopping by our country," the King said. "You are the first Europeans to stopped by our shore."

Then he assigned one of his sons, Nimely, to monitor the activities of the Europeans.

The Europeans were later taken to a lesser chief. Every country has a unique system of government and the system of the Klao leadership ran from the top to bottom. The king, as head and assisted by several sub-chiefs. Matters of lesser magnitude were decided by the sub-chiefs, while major ones were brought to the King and the Council of Elders. The Klaos never adopted any tribal societies, though they welcome those who joined from other kingdoms into their kingdom, but they never joined others. The Klaos had secret organizations— powerful in their dealings—that kept them surviving on the Grain Coast.

The Europeans met with the sub-chief. The sub-chief led the way to showing the Europeans the rest of Nana Klao, especially Jeaklon (The city). They spent a few days in the Klao Kingdom buying peppers, gold, diamonds, arts and crafts, and other valuables.

During this time, Nimely was always with them, learning their language and ways of life, repairing guns/single barrels and, learning the way they cooked their food. When the Europeans left, the king refused to install the protective covering.

"We need to trade with those people," he told his council.

Since then, whenever a European vessel docked at the port of the Klaos Kingdom, Nimely was there as a tour guide and interpreter. When there was no Europeans, the lad had his own interest. Being as curious as a child and young man, he always visited the Bassa Kingdom to be tutored by the great hunter, Boe-du. Most times he would spend weeks with Boe-du, hunting and exploring the vast and rich Bassa Forest. Upon their return, about fifty men were hired to gather the kill. Nimely also learned and understood European weapons. So, he organized a team to manufacture guns. It took he and his team about a month to produce their first gun.

The Europeans went back and forth, stopping by whenever they were on a voyage to the Orient.

All trade routes, goods and services were monitored by the local chiefs who would then report to the king. And on the contrary, that person would be severely punished and expelled from the town. Trade with the Europeans and trade amongst the communities were respected and all were to observe the rules and regulations. It provided a means of acquiring more weapons and compensations. It also provokes wars and skirmishes with other towns who tempered with this 'golden egg'.

The people learned the European language and the Europeans learned the people's language.

An incident occurred where a Grebo Chief (who depended on King Yanwleh for protection) left the set protocol and his town started trading ivory with the European at a lower price. Had it not been the Zoes who intervened, there would have been war. Another incident was the European refusal to trade with the local currency, all the towns refused to trade with the Europeans. War was declared on the Europeans. Again, the Zoes had to settle this confusion. Little did they know that the person with an advantage over another determines the course of life.

During the European stay in a town, they were free to move about and communicated freely. The king made sure to instruct a person or group of people to help them out. Besides, the rise in commercial fleets saw the increase in prices and crimes. King TappieYou was always there to assist whenever there were pirates, and during difficult times.

Man is born a mortal with a soul to aid his movement. Most time he forgets his fragility and think himself as a god. In a tragic situation, he recognizes his fragility and limitation. Yet, man is judged by the weapons of his arsenal, the powers surrounded unto him by his subjects, his relationship with the unknown, the volume of his possessions, and the fears of death in losing them all.

This great king TappieYou died at the same time as King GbeazonYou, during the year of the great harvest, immediately when the Doo Doo birds sang for the first time that afternoon. It was the first time for the rainbow to circle the moon, and for a leopard to enter the town roared four times.

As per the burial tradition, a three-week funeral ceremony was held and the following week, like his predecessors, the remains of the king were placed on top of the Samquin River. A supernatural force spins the body and like a whirlwind, his remains spin from a lower velocity to a higher one and suddenly went down into the river.

The Elders and Chief Zoes (Traditional/Spiritual heads of the kingdom) organized the turnover of power to Wleh-You, (son of Wleh), the first son and successor. He immediately instilled his brother, Nimely, as head of security. Likewise, in the Bassa country, a new king was installed by the elders. He was known as Pau-You. A few weeks after the festivities, the remaining six sons of TappieYou decided to leave the country.

Bloe travelled to the north, to the Dan country, Doeh travelled deep into the Bassa country, married the grandchild of King Gbeahzon, Tupeee, and established a town called Klao-ga-kpa (Klao people business hard) near the major trading post, Gbeah-zon, named after this great king.

The two other sons, Kon-lma-na (got blessing) and Jar-ny-wani (brought teeth) sailed to the Gold Coast. It was learned that after a few years in the Gold Coast, Jar- ywani came westward towards the Klao Kingdom where he established himself as a chief and married the daughter of the chief. His last son, Wea, settled west, the land beyond the Ten-me-ne Kingdom.

King GbarzonYou, like King TappieYou, had early contacts with the European travelers. To protect his country against possible invaders, and keeping the Bassa people together, King Pau-You added more men to the Human Leopard Society and strengthened the Neegee Society. Decreeing that only those of the society can become sub-chiefs.

He initiated King Bor-Kay and King Kpo-ken of the Dei into the society. The Mamba Bassa and the Dei recruited many young people who operated canoes services on large rivers and were reportedly involved in drowning many persons.

## THE ERA OF POWER AND STRENGTH

Dominating others has been man's greatest desire. And it doesn't matter how he achieves it, since his optimate goal is to control. Once it's obtained, power is derived, and ego displayed. Any opposing force is crushed and subdued into submission. Just like humans, nations displayed this behavior. This craving to control cuts across cultures, most made an open show of it and others congregated into organizations to protect their community.

In the pursuit of peace and protection from external threats, communities within the Green Coast established secret societies, creating what became FantaTechno. According to the inhabitants, it's not witchcraft, but a craft handed down by their forefathers, the gods, and nature itself.

FantaTechno is a combination of mystic and reality (illusion) that beats the naked eyes. It targeted the psychic to promote greatness and strength in the sight of other communities. Its main aim is to understand and bring nature into submission. Like commanding the storms, the rains, lightning and thunders, etcetera, and connecting with the spirits of the earth, water, animals, etcetera and the leaves of the forest. And every town and community had one or more of these gems. The Lorma boasted of BO and his forefathers who entered all solids. The Kissi spread the news of Kwe-tamu and his forefathers, the Lorma and Kpelleh people boasted of the Town up the Hill where everyone was borne Orthopedic surgeons, the invisible city in the Southeast of the Green Coast, the conquering of the ocean by the Krus/Klaos and rivers by the Bassas, the Gbo-yo societies of the Grebo, and so many wonders and technologies to sustain and for survival displayed by the various tribes. Each day started with someone walking in the sky, or another traveling into oblivion and bringing back goods from far away world, women bleeding continuingly because she refused a man proposal, jealous husband making wife and lover sticking together during sexual intercourse, planting live snakes in wives to deter would be lovers, and wives confessing to husbands of having several lovers, and so much more that went to the chiefs or Zoes for settlement. Everyday community displayed Fantatechnostic wizardry in the full capacity, exposing that community's capacity to other community.

Wary of these domestic concerns, all the chiefs had a conference and divided the FantaTechno societies into three categories, the borderless, communal, and local. The Borderless was established to maintain external treat and internal disturbance. Under the agreement, each native country provided men and food for the operations. They dispensed justice and were brutal in doing so. It was controlled by two Zoes from each native country, and a chief Zoe was selected to maintain order and discipline. The only Borderless society were the Human Leopard Society, Niigee, and Gboyo. Using the thickness of the jungle, the society sprang into action during the France and British Empire invasion of land east of it, trading post at the Lion Mountains, and France, south of its colony. One will wonder why the Great Powers of the West could not take that piece of land now called Liberia. The French had to skip it and went to the far east of Cape Palmas to establish a trading post for ivory while the British remained several miles away from Cape Mount.

Communal Society was established to promote cultural values, taught lessons on adulthoods, hunting and fishing, on how to remove obstacles along life journey, and healing and wellness. The Sende, Poro, Catfish, animal, and Snake societies were given those responsibilities.

The Locals were established to demonstrate tribal strengths in Juju, and technologies unique to the locale. At night children could sit by the fire hearth, and older people will tell them stories about spider and 'Sir-be-meat'. Spider stories were told to showcase heroism, greed, and mischief. Sir-be-meat, portrayed smartness, inventions, and morality. For greatness in mystical arts among the Mambah Bassa, the stories of Deh-Kpa and God-bleh Baryo ran down from generations to generations in different narratives. Deh-kpa spoke and the rain and sun obey while God-bleh Baryo commanded lightening and rain falls. Among the Lorma and Kissi of the far north, Bo and Que-tamu-Saah dominated the folklores. As previously explained, Bo and his forefathers had been the only people with the ability to enter all solid object. He would enter a large rock, and his eyes would be seen in the solid rock during the market day celebration.

As for Que-tamu-Saah, he had the ability to see witches, and chased evil things away. All the traditional countries had stories of their special heroes and it became a competition. As the stories increase, so are the heroes, and their various organizations.

Several local societies, baboon, and crocodile among others, were established, nevertheless notable among them were the Niijee of the Bassa country and Gboyoo of the Grebo country. There's one similarity and one difference between the Niijee and the Gboyoo societies. Both made their target to vanish, but the Gboyoo operated on land while the Niijee operated in water. A person targeted by the Gboyoo or Niijee would be touched by an unknown force, vanish, entered what is term as Sparto (an invisible cloud like environ), out of reality. The captured person would see and hear people talking or searching for him but unable to get to them. The only way out of Sparto, was death or insanity.

In every society, the quest is not only for political supremacy but for economic as well. Man has ventured into the unknown for economic powers but lacks the capability to translate it into a mechanism for self-reliant in their communities.

In the Grain Coast, scarcity constrained each native country to compete in the unknown for whatsoever available at the Great Door. The contestants were blind folded by a supernatural cloth, and it was incumbent on his people to cloth him with witchery or supernatural powers. Their race started at night (in their sleep) and contestants were expected by dawn. Only the strong survive, and most never made it back home.

Those who reached the door had to quickly with swiftness plunged their hands into the Great Basket with a narrow opening, pulling out whatsoever his hand lands on. If a contestant took corn, his town would harvest a lot of corn and if wished, will share it with other towns. When the Portuguese saw this massive vegetation, and when their ship drafted and docked, they were unaware of this practice and happenings.

### THE DARK AGE OF DOMINION AND SLAVERY

The Europeans continued to navigate the continent of Africa to the orient. Greed clouded their judgement and made them stone cold. And only the end (capitalism) would justify their means. All men in Europe (after seeing the light shining on the possessions of kings and the church) prepared to run the race. And no matter what it takes, they wanted to make it to the top, and getting there would be to act in the names of the king and church. The church provided spiritual conquest of the minds and submission, and the name of the king provided dominions over the inhabitants, their resources, and their existence.

When I think of the unknown, I equate it to death and the mystery surrounding it. The aftermath of life on earth; how it stuck on the psychic and makes everything on earth time bound. If everything is labelled with time, then who labels them? God! How do we know? And how many gods are there? Is there a one and only God? Are those who know this one and only God instructed by (this one and only) God to destroy the other who knows other gods? Isn't he who created those others, who are now building their individual relationships (through) the ways they know him? Then the divide, creating the morality of who's right or wrong, the killing, maiming, the burnings of God's creations at the pole, the hanging and looting, the joy it brought to the victors and the sorrow felt by the victims, the destructions and the pains, and the salvation, too good to proffer it's truly of God's works. The road it created and the world it unveiled, the diseases it unleashed, and the capitalists established, the solutions they proposed, exposing their greed and their true intention that the world was created for their sake. It was incumbent on them to spread His Word because they were the chosen race. Oh, how foolhardy men have been? The creator of the world depending on you to spread his Word through the destruction of others (God's creation)? Then, the god they know must be a god of confusion. A god who doesn't care for the poor and destitute, a god of the rich and privileges, a god of the pure in skin and a god of the capitalist. A god who doesn't care for the rest of humanity; a god who turned his face to the injustices against the weak and poor; a god who allow mass killings in his names—this god is condemned to hell.

In the name of this god and their kings, the Arabs and Europeans competed by fighting their ways to showing that they are truly chosen by God. They even created secret societies to enforce god's rules; society whose modus operandi contrary to God plans for mankind. It just showed that man's life on earth in a continual race to the top. He who gets there determines the rules for others to follow. And when his time finishes, the next group of people set the rules and on and on. The time the Europeans came, and their time clouded by profits from trade and commerce. Their interactions created the industrial revolution which needed to be fueled by human efforts. They perfected the guns to strike as many as possible at one blow. They then turned to the weak and vulnerable, disrespecting the rules set for trades and commerce, taking by force whatever was available and instituting their rules. Those who opposed were bombarded and subjugated to the will of their gods and kings. They took as many deemed necessary, they sold or resell, those taken from Africa, they forced kings and chief to surrender their own people, they kidnapped women, children, and causing conflicts amongst tribes, brothers, and sisters, holding people for ramsons, and made kings to sell their people. Then, they rewrote the story to blame the kings and chiefs. They didn't mention the kings or chiefs who resisted; they left out the part which showed the relationship between the kings, chiefs, and his subjects. They didn't mention the touch-one-touch-all principles. Yet, they didn't talk about the deep pains it left in the hearts of victims in Africa. The sorrow and sleepless nights and the tears from mothers for their children, family torn apart, and fathers feeling vulnerable and helpless, seeing his children, subjects and relatives kidnapped and taken away. It never talked about the good relationship between they and the African kings and chiefs. It didn't at all talk about the captured villages and hosting of flags in the name of their kings and their gods. In 1885, this dominance was consummated by the dividing of Africa. Again, they didn't care how family were separated, how their languages and cultures were destroyed or invalidated. The stronger force always leads the ways and set the tone. The children of Africa were taken into slavery; away from their parents to fuel the industrial revolutions and later in Africa, the children were again separated and controlled against their wills. Inventions replaced human effort. The use for slaves to fuel mass production took another turn, and people began to look at man's relationship with God from another point of view.

Generations came and went, and the issues of freedom and the rights of human made slavery an issue less attractive. But the scars, still visible, and the truth, are the hardest to accept. The fears were eminent, the writing bold and the clock ticking. As usual, the poor and impoverished population were presumed to create all the ails in society.

The diseases spread by them, the crimes committed by them, the communities ruined by them, and all the evils caused by them. But no one asked how they got to the bottom? Not a single individual stood up to say I threw them there or my diabolical behavior created this lost generation. In every city and town there were the rich and poor, and refusal of living side by side with the former masters. A picture the former masters and his offspring refuse to accept.

It became a nightmare—psychologically intolerable. Light and darkness never mixed, a verse handed down from one generation to another. But light needs darkness and the darkness needs light, a natural co-existence to create a beautiful scenery. People haunted by their egos do not see the beauty or color that comes out of mixtures. They lack that one quality, patience. The secret pill for the artist who sees the pictures before mixing the colors. When he is mixing the colors, those who don't see what he sees and are blinded by their self-images, most of the time condemn him as wasting precious time.

Because they lived in the moment, trying hard to satisfy the wanton natures and mistakes of the forefathers, they pretend to be tough. And all they see and live is failure. Failure that would ruin the nation. Failure? Yes, failure. They failed their parents and their generations. And engages in lynching to instill fears and crafted laws to justify killings that were easily avoided. But the more they did, the more the former slaves were resilient, finding comfort in the religions of their ex-masters. Which they internalized for their collective and individual survival.

The rift and rage are obvious in a country built on co-existence and freedom. It became a test for the ex-masters and the slaves themselves. It was a test of time void of solution. Void of solutions? No way: pride stood its ground. The wisest of the wises proposed solutions, calling for a separate state for ex-slaves or dumping them somewhere. Either in the Caribbean or in Africa, the land of their forefathers and cleansed them up despite the costs. Like it's said in Liberia, *a monkey cannot run away from its black hands*, these people were a United States problem, created by them and fueled by them. No one will take a woman into his home and after hundreds of years say I need you no more, get out of here. To go where? It's your problem, face it and solve it. But a call to repatriate black people to Africa was the only option, a pilot.

### THE MASTER'S SEEDS IN THE AGE OF THE PIONEERS

According to an age-old story: Mr. Joseph Cooksbutter of Kentucky was once asked by his neighbor, Jaison Goodlook, 'Among your slaves who is the most delicate and hardworking?'

'Delicate and hardworking'? Cooksbutter was sitting on his porch in his rocking chair, had a pipe stuffed with tobacco hanging down his lips; stench smell of tobacco filled the air. The white shirt looked like the dusty floor, and from a closer look at the shirt, it was covered in horse fur.

It took a few minutes for Cooksbutter to answer. He pulled the pipe from between his lips and gave it four soft hits against his trousers. Fire scattered into the air like fragments from a candle ball. The navy-blue trousers had a few tiny holes resulting from sparkles.

"My whip," Mr. Cooksbutter said, slightly turning to Jaison.

Jaison laughed. Gazing at Cooksbutter, he asked, "Are you serious?"

"The only language a slave understand is the language of the whip," Cooksbutter bragged. "The more they are whipped, the harder the slaves will work."

"Then you must be strong to work the whip," Jaison added.

"I don't work the whip; it is Samson who perform such task," Cooksbutter said, pointing to a slave who came riding on horseback.

A well-built, muscular black male disembarked the horse, ran to the porch, and bowed.

"Master," his baritone voice echoed. Trying hard not to establish eye contact with his master. A culture passed down to Samson from his late father. It was a subornation for one to look the master directly in his eyes.

"Samson punishes and works my account books," Cooksbutter bragged. "He learned fast, running the farm while I am at rest. He also runs the affairs of my house and punishes lawbreakers."

John Cooksbutter (another slave) was passing with a bag of cotton on his shoulders, heading to the barn. John eavesdropped and heard the conversation. He would still feel the impact of Samson's whip across his back. 'He's just another nigger,' he mumbled to himself. 'A house nigger who thinks he's better than us,' he continued, throwing the bundle into the one thousand two hundred seventy pounds of cottons.

John spread the news to the rest of the slaves in the field with little elaboration, adding his own version. The news spread throughout the house. It went on until the invisible line between the house and field slaves was visible and broader. The house slaves began to be respectful and loyal while the field slaves were resentful and impolite to the system.

After the civil war ended with the calls for abolition of slavery, a new page opened to the freed slaves. He had to work his way to feeding himself and family. The days of the protection of slave masters were over. The divide between the house and field were channeled into the means for survival and assimilation. Assimilation, a notion hard to accept by the slave masters or his descendants. They wanted to keep the status code to maintain their influences, wealth, and cultures of dependency. A lifestyle too hard to release. The slaves were everything to them; machine to fuel their wealth, nannies to raise their children, sex objects to satisfy their insatiable sexual appetite, beacon of powers and elitism.

Prior to this so-called emancipation, the master kept the slaves divided with the system of house slaves versus field slaves. This divide made it difficult to carry out a full rebellion. Even after slaves were given their freedom, most found it psychologically difficult to move far away from the master's residence. The masters could not stand the sight of seeing his slaves moving around without his control.

Eventually the civil war ended with the house and field slaves merging as one, becoming a common enemy for the master who could not differentiate the house from the field slaves. He instead designed a new characterization of the slaves—the pigmentation principle—the disease reddened people, those qualities that he, prior to emancipation, didn't see. The master then favors the light skin to those of darker skin. He then gave much more attention to the former than the latter.

The freed slaves' innermost desires were more than being loved and gratuity. They wanted the life of their masters; properties of their own, servants to tail their land and do domestic chores (while they swing from the hammock, cigar hanging from their lips), money to lavish and pleasures that it brought, good education, control and powers, and the social pleasures that will equate them to their former masters. They just needed that avenue, and the Grain Coast, Liberia, became that place for them to exercise that passion.

Though the United States war for independence and the civil war provided hope for former slaves, yet it began the long march to assimilation. Prior to this day, there were skirmishes, notable among those rebellions were in Haiti, Denmark, and Nat Turner.

Besides the Haiti rebellion, three mayor events led to the question of what to do with former slaves. Those major events were the Gabriel Prosser revolt in Virginia in the 1800, the Denmark Vesey in Charleston, South Carolina, and the Nat Turner rebellion in Southampton County, in Virginia, in 1831. These events shifted the thought of the slave masters to the several hundred thousand of former slaves in the various cities within the United States. Plans were crafted surgically by slave masters in the south to denigrate and demonize former slaves. Firstly, they felt it was unjust to allow their slaves to be freed. Secondly, the feeling of entitlement to this land and the direction thereof, needed to be clearly defined by them and lastly, they never wanted black people to remain in the United States. Therefore, churches and organizations were tasked with finding the solution to black men roaming the cities and streets of the United States. Ironically, those same churches who were part and parcel of the slave trade and division were now tasked with making decisions on a tiny and detested segment of the US population.

The organizations and churches made up of enslavers who still excerpted control over their loyal ex-slaves. Schools and churches were encouraged to be built to keep the enslaved confused and in submission, followed by demonizing and denigrating freed slaves. But it still did not contain the growing population of ex-slaves.

The enslavers' only hope was emancipation or a land to dump all the freed slaves. Several organizations sprung out from the churches and community.

The American Colonization Society (ACS) was one of those organizations established to manage and operationalize the plan. The British project in Freetown, (based on stories) was a success, and provided a springboard for getting black people out of the US. A team was dispatched to West Africa to ascertain the viability of a pilot project. The studies, the reports, and death did not stop the ACS from initiating the pilot. However, there were setbacks due to the terrains and mosquitoes.

Motive is always an act of the mind's construction. The British knew about Sherbro Island as the white man's grave. A place inhabited by killer insects but allowed the first group of settlers to dock. Why couldn't they allow the people to settle in Freetown? Finally, it was agreed to get a place east of Freetown.

The team meet Juin Kay-Z a former slave who had his own plan of resettling freed slaves back to Africa. Juin knew the areas and the kings, so he led the team down the Atlantic beyond Freetown to a no-go area.

## THE PROMISE LAND

Doeh, commonly referred to as Doeh-you, the great grandson of Doeh, son of Tappie-You, was installed as the new king of Klao-ga-pka. A town located near Gbeazon was established by his great grandfather.

Grudges and jealousy sicken the souls. Why grudge required payback to rest the heart, jealousy excites the heart into dangerous adventures. A man will harbor the two for a long time and will display when he has the power. Someone said, power is like a Klao/Kru canoe, rocked when you least expect, capsize in the mist of storm. Once grudge is in the hands of the bearer, it takes the heart to determine its course.

Doeh, had an age-old grudge against the Bassa King Bor-kay. The incident occurred when Bor-kay and Doeh were young men, in what is now known as Little Bassa. The former had called Klao/Kru people stupid and worthless, and Doeh accused the former of doubling dealing with the Europeans; not respecting the rules for trade and commerce set by his ancestors. When both had ascended to the positions of power, Doeh had vowed to show Bor-kay that Klao/Kru people were never stupid and worthless.

Doeh started a war with the Bassa people west of Little Bassa. His soldiers were composed mostly of former Jay-

Klays and those of other societies. This confusion started the famous forty-day war. This war involved all the tribal king-doms because of these reasons: Kinship, loots, passage, and partnership.

The rest of the Kwa group sided with King Doeh by pre-venting any intervention. It was believed that the Bassa people had enough valuables that King Bor-kay took care of. Other tribal kingdoms in the north accused him of unfair charges on goods from the north transported to the south, and his extra charges on salts. They wanted a king that would be more of a partner.

Doeh and his soldiers were enclosing on the on Bor-Kay and his men in the heart of Dugbor. A meeting was called for the next course of action, either to surrender or fight to death. While the meeting was ongoing, four boats sailed into the riv-er. These boats would determine the fate of the war between Bor-Kay and Doeh.

The strangers later paddled to the mainland and were met on arrival by several warriors of the Bassa tribe. They were ar-rested and taken to the palava hut where King Bor-Kay and his chiefs were having a discussion on how to get rid of or stop Doeh and his feared warriors from advancing to the coastline.

Juain Kay-Ze, the kingdom interpreter, was sitting in the meeting. Juain Kay-Ze was a distinguished gentleman who had extensive experience with Europeans and enough knowl-edge of the Klao Kingdom, Bassa Kingdom, Gola and Dei kingdoms and had gone to Saah-Low uncountable times. He was chosen to interrogate the intruders.

"They are looking for a place to put their people, like what happened in Saah-Low," Juain said in his local dialect.

"But where do we get land," an elder asked.

Juain ignored the elder, went to King Bor-Kay's ear and whispered something.

"Tell them we will allow them to live on Do-zon Island, if they can help us stop Doeh," the king said.

Everyone was amazed at the king's statement.

"We cannot have these people settled among us," someone objected.

"We don't know them," another said, raising an argument.

Total confusion disrupted; everyone began talking in a disorderly fashion. The king raised his hand, and the palava hut grew quiet.

"Which do you want," the king voiced. "Doeh taking this place and making us his slaves . . . or a stranger helping us, and we give a piece of land?"

The congregation remained quiet. Nobody spoke for a while.

Then an elderly man said, "These are strangers, if we gave them a piece of land to live, after a while, wouldn't they want more? Or drive us away? Look at what's happening in the Lioness Mountains?"

Everybody began staring at each other, but no one offered an answer. They all turned toward the king. He stared at the thatch roof, then back at his people.

"Let's deal with the immediate threat," the King declared.

The bombardment from the ship scared Doeh and his warriors. Killing several of his warriors and even wounding Doeh, a wound which he never survived from.

With the promise kept, a treaty was written and signed by both representatives. A European signed on behalf of the strangers while King Bor-kay put his thumbprints as signature on behalf of his people. They settled on Du-zon Island and later with the help of their armory, moved to the mainland.

Language is unique among people of like-minds and culture. With trades, commerce, and communications, one would have to learn the spoken words of those they trade with. Along the Green Coast, from the Normans to the Portuguese, the British, French and the Germans who visited or came for trade, traded in one or the other languages. Therefore, people of the Green Coast spoke multiple languages and even developed translingual words that were unique to the area. When the strangers' representatives spoke, the chiefs and others understood the language but lacked the way of transcribing it. It became their understanding that the land given and accepted through a treaty was the sole responsibility of the strangers and didn't prevent local chiefs from exercising governance over their people and trading with whomever they wanted to trade with.

As the populations of the settlers increased, they wanted more land. Already indoctrinated in the United States to spread Christianity and Civilization throughout Africa, the strangers looked at the ways of the locals as unkempt, devilish, unchristian, and uncivilized. Forgetting that the inhabitants lived on the piece of land for several centuries, under an organized governance system and well-kept cultural procedures. So, based on what they perceived the inhabitants were, their transferred to the mainland saw the desecration of scared land and places, and interfering or stopping the natives from trading with other Europeans. And in every culture, interfering with the means of survival, tempered with things that are dear to their hearts, and restricting their movement is an act of war. Soon, the settlers would learn these principles and opt for independence.

The strangers had their protectors in the distance land and were protected by white people. The white men did the dirty work for the strangers to settle on the land to become their country. A kindness the strangers will acknowledge but refused to allow people (white men) of his skin color to legally live alongside them. There was a white man, who the inhabitant had respect for named, Jehudi Ashmun. Though a representative of the strangers placed there by the United States, but he had a special relationship with the locals. He learned their language and went to them when he needed answers to the lands and spirits of the lands. It was Ashmun who went to the locals to learn about the seasons, and about the right time to plant crops. Though a white man, he had special connections with the people of the Green Coast, Recaptured slaves, and others from the Caribbean and those from neighboring countries, all settled in Liberia.

Several years later, the commonwealth became Liberia and a government was set up. Years later, the government needed resources and the locals had enough in their communities. Subsequent government strategized ways to get the locals and their communities under the control of Monrovia. Propagandas passed by word of mouth on the atrocities committed by France and Great Britain, and the locals gave into the demands of Monrovia, and the commissioner's system, back by the Liberian Frontier Forces which brought the locals into total submission.

The battles for the soul of the land

"We can't win this war," Garpue said, after crawling at the feet of King Dwezoom. He was breathing heavily and sweating all over his shirtless body. His right hand clanged to his spear, kneeling one knee on the dusty sand of the city of Warch.

King Dwezoom didn't move but continued staring at the many wounded worriers spread under the Palava Hut of the mighty healer Kamu. The King pretended as if he had not heard Garpue.

"They are being helped by witches of the sea," Garpue said, referring to the United States gun boats on the sea. "We almost drove them out, my King," Garpue added, attempting to motivate the depressed king.

"What do you want us to," the king asked.

Garpue responded, "You are my king; we will lay our lives down for you and this land," he assured.

"Gather the council together," the king stood and ordered. "I want everyone to meet me right now in the secret bush!"

Garpue passed the king's word to the Town Cryer and immediately followed the gathering to the Secret Bush.

The Council gathered in the inner chamber of the Secret Bush; a place meant for top secrets of the land. Garpue stood attentively within hearing distance. While the war rage on, the council debated for nearly an hour, without coming to a compromise on three keys issues: those who wanted to fight to death, those who called for collaboration with other kingdoms to defend the land, and those who called for an end to the carnage and live alongside the settlers. The king had to make the final decision.

With everyone's eyes fixated on the king, he stood, took in his breath, and let it out.

"Once the people have the witch of the sea on their side, we can't win this war," the king pronounced. "Just one shout from her mouth, and thousands of our people are wounded! If we call other kingdoms into our war, it shows our weakness. These people continue to dig into our land, and they won't stop. They took our biggest traditional bush and cleared it out to build their Secret Bush to worship their gods. Like a mighty wind, they are indoctrinating our children into foreign ideas, while our children are dropping our ways of life. This move is a slow poison, and we must blame it on our forefathers. Right now, there is no time for blame. It's time for us to save our people and what is left of us. Let it be told that we want to meet the white man for a peace talk!"

The gathering mumbled in agreement.

An eight-man delegation was immediately set up to broker peace with the settlers. They met with Judi Ashmun, and he agreed to meet with the king in the city of Warch.

Ashmun went to the meeting with a case of smoked fish, smoked pork, and several bottles of rum. The meeting lasted for four hours and in the end, it was agreed that they live alongside one another in peace, exchanging ideas and strategies for survival.

When Ashmun returned, there was opposition who greeted the agent with disapproval. They wanted the war to continue, they wanted King Dwezoon to be prosecuted and hanged, and they wanted more land. However, Ashmun refused, which was his greatest mistake.

The settlers were divided into segments: dark skin and mulatto (a racial classification to refer to people of mixed African and European ancestry). Underlying that division were those with multiples of other problems; those who wanted inclusivity by bringing in the natives and having one country, and those who wanted an all-settlers republic by living along the Atlantic Ocean without the natives. They had returned to Africa with a mind of revenge, a mind to pay back for being sold into slavery and wanted to pay back on any African.

This segment of the settlers and their descendants were boisterous and were lucky to be in the echelon of powers, considering the natives beneath them in every form of civilization. Feeling entitled to the land and the resources while denying the inhabitants (the true owners) every right to better their lives. Instead, they outsourced the resources for little money or goods to build Monrovia and buy houses abroad, stored huge sums of money for their descendants in foreign banks while the natives remained in abject poverty.

They also made the history of the natives, hidden from them—no mentioned of their kings or queens or strongmen. They allowed these people to linger in a state of oblivion, badmouth their ways of lives, societies, and secret societies, but held unto and cherished those societies from the white man's land.

These colonizers copied the life of the slave masters by enslaving the natives, making them to work for them while they relaxed in comfort. Though they were in Africa, their minds were still enslaved in the United States: the dress-code, customs and traditions, language, the system of government (which they never understood), named their habitats after where they were enslaved, even drawing a line between they and the native, calling themselves the civilized and the natives, heathen.

This half-educated segment of the colonizers wanted an all-settlers republic; hating the white man and hating the natives (preferring the former to the latter), but they never rejected the white man's donations, help, and those of the primitive people. They spent their time on their porches refusing to work but daydreaming of the place that refused to allow black people be humans. These semi-schoolers and hate-driven group went after Ashmun, demonizing him. They refused to be mingled with these recaptured slaves, neither to live among them, and was instrumental in destroying the royal system of government that existed among the natives and made sure to never write about the traditions and customs of the natives, making them invisible.

This segment changed the African names of the natives who wanted to be educated, and in the end, they became selected a few families who ruled Liberia towards the ends of the twentieth Century. The same tactic the slave masters used on the black people in the United States. An unthinkable irony and mistake.

There were skirmishes as the natives fought back, but Uncle Sam gun boats and stockpiles of weapons continue to give the colonizers the edge. The natives gave into fears, became numbed to the activities of the Frontier Forces backed by Monrovia—hanging and killing of kings and queens, destruction of traditions and customs, taking of land and disrespect of sacred places, denial of citizenship to natives, and looting of resources given to foreigners for kickbacks—to build Monrovia and send their children abroad while natives remained in poverty. These are the evidence of the diabolical attacks carry out by United States and backed by the colonizers.

# Chapter 1

Never given to understatement, Jules had announced his intentions from the very first day. Whether Naomi had considered him or not, he wasn't going to take any chances.

"Are you the girl with the message?" he asked.

She thought for a moment about how she wanted to answer.

"Could you step this way, sir?"

What we may term "prescientific days" people were in no uncertainty about the interpretation of dreams. When they were recalled after awakening they were regarded as either the friendly or hostile manifestation of some higher powers, demoniacal and Divine. With the rise of scientific thought the whole of this expressive mythology was transferred to psychology; to-day there is but a small minority among educated persons who doubt that the dream is the dreamer's own psychical act.

But since the downfall of the mythological hypothesis an interpretation of the dream has been wanting. The conditions of its origin; its relationship to our psychical life when we are awake; its independence of disturbances which, during the state of sleep, seem to compel notice; its many peculiarities repugnant to our waking thought; the incongruence between its images and the feelings they engender; then the dream's evanescence, the way in which, on awakening, our thoughts thrust it aside as something bizarre, and our reminiscences mutilating or rejecting it—all these and many other problems have for many hundred years demanded answers which up till now could never have been satisfactory.

Before all there is the question as to the meaning of the dream, a question which is in itself double-sided. There is, firstly, the psychical significance of the dream, its position with regard to the psychical processes, as to a possible biological function; secondly, has the dream a meaning—can sense be made of each single dream as of other mental syntheses?

Three tendencies can be observed in the estimation of dreams. Many philosophers have given currency to one of these tendencies, one which at the same time preserves something of the dream's former over-valuation. The foundation of dream life is for them a peculiar state of psychical activity, which they even celebrate as elevation to some higher state. Schubert, for instance, claims: "The dream is the liberation of the spirit from the pressure of external nature, a detachment of the soul from the fetters of matter." Not all go so far as this, but many maintain that dreams have their origin in real spiritual excitations, and are the outward manifestations of spiritual powers whose free movements have been hampered (Aristotle, 340 BC)("Dream Phantasies," Scherner, Volkelt). A large number of observers acknowledge that dream life is capable of extraordinary achievements—at any rate, in certain fields ("Memory").

In striking contradiction with this the majority of medical writers hardly admit that the dream is a psychical phenom-

enon at all. According to them dreams are provoked and initiated exclusively by stimuli proceeding from the senses or the
body, which either reach the sleeper from without or are ac-
cidental disturbances of his internal organs.

The dream has no greater claim to meaning and importance than the sound called forth by the ten fingers of a person
quite unacquainted with music running his fingers over the
keys of an instrument. The dream is to be regarded, says Binz,
"as a physical process always useless, frequently morbid." All
the peculiarities of dream life are explicable as the incoherent
effort, due to some physiological stimulus, of certain organs,
or of the cortical elements of a brain otherwise asleep.

But slightly affected by scientific opinion and untrou-
bled as to the origin of dreams, the popular view holds
firmly to the belief that dreams really have got a meaning,
in some way they do foretell the future, whilst the meaning
can be unravelled in some way or other from its oft bizarre
and enigmatical content. The reading of dreams consists in
replacing the events of the dream, so far as remembered,
by other events. This is done either scene by scene, according to some rigid key, or the dream as a whole is replaced
by something else of which it was a symbol. Serious-mind-
ed persons laugh at these efforts—"Dreams are but sea-
foam!"

"That's not what he said," Cindy replied.

"I don't care. Do it anyway."

"Okay, boss, here I go."

With that, she walked out of the office.

One day I discovered to my amazement that the popular view grounded in superstition, and not the medical one,
comes nearer to the truth about dreams. I arrived at new
conclusions about dreams by the use of a new method of psy-
chological investigation, one which had rendered me good

service in the investigation of phobias, obsessions, illusions, and the like, and which, under the name "psycho-analysis," had found acceptance by a whole school of investigators. The manifold analogies of dream life with the most diverse conditions of psychical disease in the waking state have been rightly insisted upon by a number of medical observers.

It seemed, therefore, a priori, hopeful to apply to the interpretation of dreams methods of investigation which had been tested in psychopathological processes. Obsessions and those peculiar sensations of haunting dread remain as strange to normal consciousness as do dreams to our waking consciousness; their origin is as unknown to consciousness as is that of dreams.

It was practical ends that impelled us, in these diseases, to fathom their origin and formation. Experience had shown us that a cure and a consequent mastery of the obsessing ideas did result when once those thoughts, the connecting links between the morbid ideas and the rest of the psychical content, were revealed which were heretofore veiled from consciousness. The procedure I employed for the interpretation of dreams thus arose from psychotherapy.

This procedure is readily described, although its practice demands instruction and experience. Suppose the patient is suffering from intense morbid dread. He is requested to direct his attention to the idea in question, without, however, as he has so frequently done, meditating upon it. Every impression about it, without any exception, which occurs to him should be imparted to the doctor.

The statement that will be perhaps then made, that he cannot concentrate his attention upon anything at all, is to be countered by assuring him most positively that such a blank state of mind is utterly impossible. As a matter of fact, a great number of impressions will soon occur, with which others will associate themselves. These will be invariably accompanied by the expression of the observer's opinion that they have no meaning or are unimportant. It will be at once noticed that it is this self-criticism that prevented the patient from imparting the ideas, which had indeed already excluded them from consciousness. If the patient can be induced to abandon this self-criticism and to pursue the trains of thought which are yielded by concentrating the attention, most significant matter will be obtained, matter which will be presently seen to be clearly linked to the morbid idea in question. Its connection with other ideas will be manifest, and later on will permit the replacement of the morbid idea by a fresh one, which is perfectly adapted to psychical continuity.

This is not the place to examine thoroughly the hypothesis upon which this experiment rests, or the deductions which follow from its invariable success. It must suffice to state that we obtain matter enough for the resolution of every morbid idea if we especially direct our attention to the unbidden associations which disturb our thoughts—those which are otherwise put aside by the critic as worthless refuse. If the procedure is exercised on oneself, the best plan of helping the experiment is to write down at once all one's first indistinct fancies.

I will now point out where this method leads when I apply it to the examination of dreams. Any dream could be made use of in this way. From certain motives I, however, choose a dream of my own, which appears confused and meaningless to my memory, and one which has the advantage of brevity. Probably my dream of last night satisfies the requirements. Its content, fixed immediately after awakening, runs as follows.

"Company; at table or table d'hôte . . . .. Spinach is served. Mrs. E.L., sitting next to me, gives me her undivided attention, and places her hand familiarly upon my knee. In defense I remove her hand. Then she says: 'But you have always had such beautiful eyes." I then distinctly see something like two eyes as a sketch or as the contour of a spectacle lens."

# Chapter 2

Huge cheers awaken Gonganue, who is said to have fallen into a supernatural unconsciousness, and still couldn't believe how he got there. He was in the presence of Maxi Moore, tied to a pole, near scaffolds. Seven men wearing palm straws, their faces marked with chalks, holding spears, bows, and arrows, surround him in a ring, yelling and doing the Grebos' war dance. He still had no idea how he was taken out of Sall Pue and brought back to his town, in his kingdom. He trembled upon seeing his wives and children seated opposite Maxi Moore, all the sub chiefs on the left of Maxi Moore. The reality came upon that something was wrong. The power of his charms had dwindled; the strength of his heritage had fallen so low. Gonganue then knew that his end was near. Never in his lifetime or those of his ancestors, the Dan, charms, and power second to none. According to the great healer, Oldman Gondah, the power belonging to the Dan would scatter because of control and greed. But Gonganue did not know that it would happen during his reign. Oldman Gondah's prophecy was like a fairytale and never taken seriously. Now, he was in the presence of Maxi Moore, and the commander of the Commissioner, with whom he had had quarrels, seated a few meters from Maxi Moore. His face was lighted, beaming with smile.

The people from the town—men separated from women—was on the right. The soldiers lined up, kneeling, and pointing their guns at them. Children crawled and held tightly to the knees of their mothers, crying.

"Shut up!" Maxi Moore's voice thundered.

The children hushed immediately.

Maxi Moore looked toward Commissioner Zarkay, and he stood.

"I want to thank Commander Mazizizi," the Commissioner said, struggling with pronouncing the name.

Maxi Moore nodded and motioned him to continue.

"Our Grebo brother, thank you," he said, smiling from ear to ear. "This new spiritual force called 'Boe-yoe' is so powerful that it can bring anyone from the hidden places to the known," he continued. "This man," he looked at Gonganue and pointed.

Gonganue looked up at him, shaking his head in disappointment.

"Has done great evil," Commissioner Zarkay continued. "I am a living witness. He killed a soldier out of jealousy. Look at her,' he pointed at Kou. "She used her charms on the corporal just as she has done to him. She doesn't deserve to be sitting there, but with him, set to be hung. I rest my case," he finished and took his seat.

The noose was checked one last time and strengthened. Gonganue's indigenous gown was removed, his arms bounded behind his back, and the rope placed around his neck.

Maxi Moore turned to Gonganue. "Why did you kill my Corporal," he asked him.

"I caught him sleeping with my wife," Gonganue replied.

"You killed a soldier because he laid with your wife," Commander Moore asked.

"She's my head wife, and that is against our laws."

"So, what?" Maxi Moore shouted, looking at his men.

A burst of laughter followed.

"You will be hung, and your wife is mine now. . . your children will be property of this town. The laws of Liberia supersede all other laws. Your laws do not give you the right to take the life of a Liberian citizen," Maxi Moore added.

The hangman took hold of the pole and the lever, ready to perform what command would be given him.

"Wait," Maxi Moore ordered. He motioned the interpreter to ask Gonganue, "Any last words?"

After the interpreter had spoken, Gonganue lifted his head, and looked at his wives and children. Nobody was crying; his children were at the feet of their mothers, holding on like one holding a pole.

"Our forefathers told us to welcome you for our safety," Gonganue said. "We gave you food. . .our young men cleared the road for your passage and transported you on their shoulders to various native countries and across dangerous waters. . . even fought alongside you. Yet, you take our wives. Why?"

"Liberia is a country of laws," Maxi Moore declared, pointing at Gonganue. "Your country is enjoying our freedom and security. Therefore, you are to abide by all our laws. Killing is breaking the laws of Liberia. . . and killing a soldier of the Frontier Force, a citizen, makes it even worst. By directive of the President of Liberia, I hereby sentenced you to death by public hanging!"

"Your soldier broke our laws," Gonganue shouted back. "Our punishment is death for a non-citizen."

"I am not a citizen of your country," Gonganue said. "Why are you imposing your laws upon me? Your forefathers promised that we would maintain our independence. Our country forbids 'running after' someone else's wife, and having a love affair is death to the man and the woman. It's our country and our laws, and you are in my country."

"Your country is within my country," Maxi Moore said. "Although you are not a citizen of my country, we provide you protection and care, which subject you to our jurisprudence. Hang him now! Enough of this nonsense!"

The hangman pulled the lever and Gonganue's body sunk immediately below the misfit scaffold. His legs jerked, swaying left to right, body exerting more wight on the noose, tightening it. In a few minutes, his body came to a stop. Gonganue's head tilted sideways, and his tongue stuck out.

The killing of Gonganue ended the Dan dynastic. The Republic of Liberia strategy to indirectly rule the interiors was to have the president select and install commissioners. Puppet chiefs were replaced with commissioners who became Monrovia's whips to bring their own people into submission. Living as the representatives of the President of Liberia, the values and powers that came with it places commissioners above the chiefly or kingly arrangement that was the order of the day. The little money from Monrovia and the comfort of getting anything from the locals made the position of commissioner a contested one. Juju and human or animals' sacrifices became the means of maintaining power, being feared, getting rid of contenders, and doing anything to win Monrovia favors.

A commissioner took over the Dan Country. He took Gonganue's wives as his, incorporated former nobles into the government farms, pilot project and exposed his people innermost secrets, just everything to maintain power. It worked for the Republic of Liberia, and similar strategy was implemented in other parts of the country, giving the Republic of Liberia grips on the entire land mass.

Someone once said, to know the true character of a person gives him power and money. As for me, I believe to know the true character of a man, let his power come from a superior power.

The Republic of Liberia, founded by outcasts of the United States of America in search of a place to call home—due to the injustice they faced in the US because of the color of their skin—landed on this these shores of greenness and potential penniless and devastated. Once permitted on an island and later, on the mainland, learned survival skills from the natives, drew a line and pushed the natives to the side. The discrimination is not on the color of the skin but on civilization and economic wellbeing. Coming from the US, they considered themselves highly developed and civilized, pushing the natives to the side and the methods used to keep them in check spoke otherwise. When the Republic advance into the interior through lies and fears, they never meant to create a nation of freed people, harnessing their individual cultures into a single whole, but they created a nation for themselves, and fear of extinction, created a culture of exclusivity, taking the natives natural resources for themselves, building a Monrovia for themselves and sending their children abroad for advance education to continue the system. Therefore, maintaining a grip on the natives, the commissioners (natives own greedy kinsmen) and the Frontier Forces (militia group aided by Great Britain and US). This newly found source of power turned commissioners into monsters, a payback on chiefs and their families, a source of acquiring goods and services, owning large farms, livestock, and land, domestic servants, marrying women (married or unmarried) and, getting at the husbands and anyone who refuses to give his daughters into wedlock. Commissioners were powerful because of the supports from Monrovia and the Liberia Frontier Forces.

# Chapter 3

Although the town chief and king of Zeonplay, Gonganue Dan was also a hunter, he graduated from the famous Tarpet's School of hunting, in the forest of Tarpet Town. Zeonplay, a town in the Dan Country, situated near the border of Tchien, is about 1.67 square miles. Its population of 5,392 regulated the social, commercial, and political activities in both the Dan and Krahn Countries. Both countries had a combined population of 524,798.

Gonganue was the most feared chief, ruling his household and subjects in an uncompromising manner. He possessed six wives; four as a token of peace from those subordinate chiefs, and the last one, Kou, a wife acquired through a display of supernatural power. Kou was his head wife, and favorite. It was believed that she was the most beautiful woman in Zeonplay. Others described her as the shining moon, bright into the morning hours.

Individually, each wife had her hut and was supplied food on a weekly basis. They took term visiting his quarter, but the children could visit their father at any time. The children always look forward to such a time because it offered an intimate moment with the father. At the fire hearth, he told them stories about his participation in warfare, hunting experience especially hunting lions, tigers, and elephants. At that time, the chief would tell stories about his forefathers and suspenseful and supernatural happenings during their reign. He also gives them straightforward instructions about manhood. Gonganue also used that time to handle all complaints and disciplined each child.

Girls were under their mothers' complete control, and the society mandated it as her duties to bring a girl child up in dignified and serviceable manners. Each wife manages her own household, and during her term to fulfill her conjugal duty at the palace it was when she would tell her husband (The Chief) about other matters like women and community matters.

All a wife was, a mother organizing her domestic affairs, and looking forward to her term in meeting her husband demands. Communication was only limited to 'hello, where is my food, is my bath water ready?' Except during the time for a husband to know his wife, a wife will have the privilege to discuss other matters.

As per tradition, it was deemed cowardice and of a weak nature for a man to be control by his wife. Discussing a man's daily experience with his wife was forbidden.

Women only source of recreation and entertainment was at the creeks where they went to fetch water, had opportunity to discuss women issues, got updated version of gossips from each household and the towns, and during the feast celebrating harvest when they do a lot of dancing and dining.

Chief Gonganue gave special privilege to traditional healers; they could practice their crafts in any community. He decreed that all master storytellers within the length and breadth of the kingdom open nightly fire hearth storytelling sections to educate young people about their customs and traditions.

The legendary spider whose name was familiar throughout the Klao Kingdom and other kingdoms far and near, was used in stories to teach morals and escape strategies. Land was for the community, not the people because people died but the community won't and was forbidden to be sold. Anyone who wanted a piece of the land for farming or to build, was instructed to go to his chief or the king.

King visited each other and during a king's visit, it was the opportunity to showcase his kingdom's power and resources. Two notable tales were when King Yanwleh went to visit the great-great-grandfathers of Sua CoCo and Bo Swain in Central Grain Coast. According to legend the King's attendants (young and beauty women) spread gold dust from the Klaos Kingdom to their destination. Twenty gigantic men took terms transporting the king, using his mobile house. The dancing divas moved according to the drummer's tempo and the serenaded voices of the court musicians. It was during that journey that the Klaos people developed a classical version of the Gbema, done in a soul touching fashion. They sang praises to the king, and the greatness of the Klaos people, their conquests, and technologies.

When it was time for those kings to visit King Yanwleh, they took along magicians, a lot of food, shining stones (diamonds), friendship and goodwill. Thereafter, these visits became common, a tradition, and it connected the different kingdoms and people.

Like subsistence farming, power shifted from one kingdom to another. The kingdom with an abundance of food, plenty of women, the opportunity to make a farm and build a house for oneself, and a leadership that provided protection for its people attracted more manpower. These qualities strengthened a kingdom's way to the top. At the top, power and influence distinguish it from others and unconsciously resist external forces.

For Zeonplay to be considered the central trading center in the North Central, Gonganue won a lot of critical physical and spiritual battles. He contained the arrogance of Chief Gayeh in Tchien, in the town east of his province and replaced him with his slave, Zoe Gbah. He took away Keh, who was betroth to Gayeh. Gayeh's family didn't take kindly to Gonganue's attitude.

He disciplined Chief Payeyou of the Maah, in the south of his province, and installed the town herbalist Kpah Du as chief. He fought and killed in his dreams, Chief Manbu and Kerkuree in the west and north, destroying their legacy by replacing them with sub-Chiefs Mamadee and Superee, who were of lower status. When he was settled and comfortable with his surroundings, Gonganue crafted several laws: instructing all produce from those towns to be brought to Zeonplay for sales. Each town was mandated to provide service men for the communal farms, taking another man's life and stealing were forbidden, and coveting another man's wife was an abomination.

He set time for territorial meetings where all the other chiefs would come to Zeonplay for a meeting and for a feast. He also decreed those disputes of greater magnitude threatening the security of his territorial boundaries and those of the sub-chiefs were brought to him for settlement.

He re-organized the Human Leopard and Snake Societies out of the Poro society, operating under distinct mandates. Though different from the past Leopard and snake societies modernized. The Human Leopard Society was like a police organization, arresting adversaries in the bush or forest and humiliating them for various reasons. Its members wore Leopard skin to look like Leopards and through a magical means deal with his/ her victims. The society further strengthened Gonganue's relationship with many chiefs among the Mende, Temne, Belle, Lorma, Kissi and Gbandi.

The Snake Society was mainly organized for entertainment purposes. Its membership was made of both men and women whose tamed snakes, and during feasts or if the town received special guests, they play and dance with the snakes.

Gonganue and his head wife, Kou, had a yearly travel plan where they would go to the Khondoh Kingdom to visit its great king, Mansagee Sao Boso. During his realm, Mansagee Sao Boso was the great ruler of the Bola, Lorma, Kpelleh, Gbandi and Mandingo tribes in the Khondoh Kingdom. During their visit, he was enrolled into the Mornigii, a magical association while his wife joined the Zarzay and the Koloi. The Zarzay teaches a woman how to dance and sing while the Koloi was organized especially for fraternal purposes.

While in the Khondoh kingdom, Gonganue was amazed as well as admired the political system of the Lorma people. Their system was centralized, though, not under a single ruler, but under a series of chiefs or kings who were heads of autonomous clans or regions. During his meeting with the great king, Gonganue learned from him that mostly his people migrated from the ancient kingdom of Mali. He was told that after several fights among the leaders of Mali, many people fled with one of the defeated aspirants to the throne, whom they referred to as Faili Khama.

Gonganue also visited several other kingdoms, including the Gola, Dey, Bassa, and those along the coastline and further east. He made sure to applied most of what he learned from his travels to govern his people and made sure to build relationship with kings and chiefs.

During harvest, Gonganue ordered all sub-chiefs to present him with gifts of different food stuffs on a seasonal basis.

Zeonplay was a town connecting several other towns resembling or showing it as a kingdom where Gonganue Dan was the overseer. Over a period, Zeonplay became a major trading post in the north, receiving traders and visitors from the Kpelleh Kingdom, Lorma Kingdom, Bassa Kingdom, Gola Kingdom and several great kingdoms along the coastal areas. With all the glory, Zeonplay was envied by the other native countries and its chief, feared.

Gonganue's people and other countries believe he had extra supernatural powers. The power that would make him disappear and discerned any plans to assassinate him. His body was tattooed and his cow tail he carried daily was meant to subdue his opponent. The entire country knew that he got the cow tail from his late mother through a dream. The charms and the stories that went with it made him a proud king and a hunter, and people bow when they saw him. He was the only chief king who resisted the Republic of Liberia's influence within the tribal countries. His forefathers have allowed Liberia in for security, and he respected their words to the republic. But he opposed the republic's tempering with their politics and cultures.

However, with all the power and authority, one thing he lacked was spending time with his family. His daily life was devoted to the affairs of his people. Though each wife had allotted time with him, none of those times were intimate enough to fill his wife's loneliness and unhappiness. Moreover, it was unthinkable for one within that culture to go after the chief wives.

# Chapter 4

## THE COMMUNAL SYSTEM AND THE CURSE

Just like the rest of Africa, the Grain Coast was still living and operating a communal philosophy and economic system. Everything belongs to the people and was regulated higher powers, and men aided in maintaining its security. Land was accepted as a gift from the higher power to support men daily journey on earth and never to be sold; the forest believed to provide and support wellness and food never to be destroyed or misused; gold was for royalty and only the best of smiths could beat it into his imagination; diamonds thought to be spiritual and only harnessed by great men; and so forth.

Overtime a monetary system replaced the barter system. Money was used strictly for transaction of goods and services provided by humans. It was never meant for the purchase of land and water. Land and water were given by the gods for the benefit of everyone in the community, though the community but regulated by the Zoes. Accordingly, it was forbidden for a chief or king to discuss cases pertaining to land. If a stranger wanted a space to farm or build his house, he asked the chief, describing the kind of farm and the type of house. The chief would discuss it with the Zoes, and a space would be given to that person if approved. That is how important land was and control; free but one must ask. Money was never valuable enough to purchase the people's land. History taught us to believe Bob Gray sold the people's land for 'smoked fish.' Smoked fish? How possible? It sounds easy, but the infamous Robert F. Stockton had to use a gun. Is his story true? Well, the land was sold or donated.

Over time, the communal practice along the coastal areas were influenced and corroded by the European culture of land acquisition. Lots of Europeans stopped by to trade with the locals. Gold, diamonds, and other gems that were considered precious and left alone, were stolen through European influence for a token of appreciation. It is known that a value of a thing is determined by its scarcity and knowledge of its worth. But in a primitive society that lacks knowledge, even if a valuable is in abundance, will find ways to connect those valuables to a higher power just to protect it.

The European knew the values (in monetary terms) of gold, diamonds, and other valuables so they influence a trusted local to stealing those valuables for rewards.

# Chapter 5

The Elizabeth, of the American Colonization Society (ACS), departed New York harbor on February 6, 1820 and sailed to West Africa with eighty-six passengers. Then in 1821 and 1838, more people came to the settlement to be called Liberia.

The Altingtons were amongst those who came in 1821. These twin brothers (mulatto) came to Liberia through "stow way" and were not listed. Their actions in the war between the native's countries for settlement on the mainland had them noted by the ACS, John and Samuel Altington, came from a plantation in Northern Virginia, ran away from their slave masters to New York, paid the guard at dock and sailed to West Africa. They hailed from a family who were good-looking and charming, married their way into the upper class of the Monrovian aristocracy, befriending Jehudi Ashmun, after the death of his wife.

Ashmun was born on April 21, 1794, at a farm near Champlain, New York. A theologian and journalist, Ashmun sailed to West Africa, along with his wife in 1822. Upon his arrival in

Monrovia in August of that year, the colony was without supplies, leadership, and constant threat from angry tribes. What really brought the misunderstanding? Did the tribes feel cheated during the negotiation settlers occupied? Did Freetown show a good example of colonization that had the locals thinking twice?

Though the tribes were angry over a group of people settling on their land, the settlers (whose ancestors) once lived on this land (continent of Africa) felt equally entitled. But did the negotiators sell the idea that the returnees were long-lost children of Africa who chose to return? Or did they tell the returnees that the occupiers were relatives of their forefathers? Maybe the stories were narrated differently to the two groups. Maybe they told different stories (separately and in secretly) that sowed divisions and mistrust. Or fears emulating from the Ashanti wars in the Gold Coast and the takeover of the Lioness Mountains and the injustices that accompanied it, were too good an example to overlook. On one hand the settlers were welcomed, on the other hand, the locals were suspicious of these group of people especially being led by 'white people,' those who had them subjugated to a prolonged period of slavery. So, they rebelled consistently; but were met with resistance from the gunboats stationed off the coast. These smashes from the locals left the settlers in disarray. When Ashmun reached the colony, he met the colony disorganized, and he chose to help in preserving the colony.

"We need to organize ourselves to protect this God-giving Land," Ashmun said to one of the Altington brothers.

"Who does he think he is," they questioned in their minds.

"Has he forgotten that he's on the land of our forefathers," Samuel mumbled to John, knowing that he wanted to reply to this white man who was extending his authority across the Atlantic Ocean.

"I feel like this is where I belong," Ashmun declared to Samuel. "I can feel it! Therefore, I must defend it with my blood. . . for us and our generations."

John and Samuel stood speechless. They stared at him until he was out of sight, following Elijah Johnson to the governor's quarter.

Johnson was the acting governor of the colony. He took over from Frederick James who acted as governor for three months. James was the first Black acting agent who succeeded Eli Ayers.

Elijah Johnson and the Altington brothers organized men and women for the successful defense of the colony. After the fight, Ashmun began envisioning a United States empire in Africa. He began purchasing or taking land and expanding the colony. He forced the settlers to work hard, and those who refused were denied food. It was one of the Altington boys who said Ashmun always felt that whenever he was in the colony, he felt like he was home. He wanted a place to call home for his generations.

According to oral history, Ashmun cheated death many times. Notable among them was during a fight when he was captured by the fierce native Bassa chief. The chief allowed him to go, stating that the oracle said Ashmun's life must be spared because he was son of the soil.

In as much as he was successful in calming down the hostilities, some in the colony did not like his style of leadership. He was ousted and fled to Cape Verde Island. A negotiation team came in and Ashmun was restored. Ashmun dream of establishing a United States empire in Africa was not realized.

He felt sick and traveled back to the United States, where he died.

Corporal Jeremiah Altington was the fifth generation of the Altingtons, inheriting all these qualities. Having an uncle, Chief Justice of the young republic, made Commander Maxi Moore very careful.

His entry into Zeonplay and seeing the chief wife for the first time lighted a craving within him for her. He started surprising her with clothing and sweet perfume from Monrovia, telling her stories about the city, the buildings and about amazing things. He started having an affair with her. The first time he slept with her, Gonganue felt like something left him. His visit to the scared bush, and his return to her compound, Kou started confessing, telling her husband about her affairs with Corporate Altington. Gonganue wasted no time but took his single barrel gun, marched to the station, and shot the corporal. The corporal died instantly, and when he realized what had happened, he flew into the bush.

People always said it was the last straw that broke the camel back. This was Gonganue's last straw. Liberia needed him out to take complete control of the native countries, and his opponents also wanted him out, so they ganged up against him. He was hung and killed. Fearing a collective judgement, most of the Dans changed their names to settlers' names. Only a few maintained the original name.

After a few years, Firestone Rubber and Tire company wanted laborers for its rubber plantations near Monrovia and in Cavalla, in Maryland. The Dans were amongst those forced out of their land and taken to clear the land for Firestone. When December has come, the intermittent whirlwind swirling freely, driving away everything in its path into nothingness so is what happened to the people of the Grain Coast after the takeover of the Republic of Liberia. Kings and people of reputation were reduced to ordinary. An entire dynasty was intentionally erased; the history of the natives stopped being forgotten, but the history of the settlers was recorded to prove their superiority.

A new group of people who had no time to submit to authority replaced the traditional hegemony to change the course of history. Over a period, it has driven the people into their individual tribal enclaves for protection and unity, and the demarcation of the landmass into territories based on tribes worsened the divides. People preferred to blindly be aligned with their kinsmen than people from other tribes. A lot of people linked themselves to their tribes as opposed to identifying with Liberia. Most have not realized that they belong to Liberia and all the tribes and tribal countries make up Liberia. Many people feel comfortable being refer to as being a part of a tribal region or tribe, then saying 'I am a Liberian'.

It is noted that the only time someone would say they are from Liberia, is when they find themselves in a foreign country. Because in those places, the people don't know the various tribes, but a country called Liberia. Tribalism is one of the greatest opponents of unity and unification in Liberia.

# Chapter 6

It was a foggy December morning in 1978, the haze overshadowed the Duport Road Community in Paynesville, spreading its wings like puffs of smoke. It precipitated into tiny bits of flakes wetting the habitation. Nevertheless, this wetness couldn't stop the four ladies who were out in the wet, monitoring four huge pots sitting on the fire hearths. The smell of Palm Butter and Potatoes Green soups filled the air, as well as the scent from the mixture of cooked Pusawa rice and Jollof Rice. The ladies were dancing and singing to Liberia's Morris Dorley 'Who are you baby?' The smell of alcohol was evident because a large bottle containing cane juice soaked in roots and spice and two large bottles of Kontiki Gin boosted their energy to cook the food.

The dancing and singing attracted the neighbors, and a few sneaked into the Rogers' yard to see the dancing ladies. Their actbegang of a grand celebraion, commemorating the graduation of Frank Dan from the College of West Africa.

Frank Dan was still in his room seated, already dressed awaiting his godfather, Mr. Joshua Rogers', returned from the Sinkor Shopping Center to take him to the school auditorium, the convocation hall.

The festivity in the kitchen was much louder now, it attracted Frank. He walked to the window and drew the curtain in a small proportion that nobody could see him peeping. He saw the ladies doing their thing and smiled to himself.

Frank went over to his study desk directly underneath an oval-shaped mirror, opened the drawer, and took out a sheet of paper. He lifted his head and was surprised at his appearance. He had grown muscular. The early morning push-ups had reshaped his upper arms and shoulders and were made visible by the slim fitted white shirt and neatly netted black tie that snaked around his neck and down his chest.

He had looked into the mirror several times, but that was the only time he had truly seen himself looking so splendid. It had him wondering where did he got this physique and good looks? Frank had never known his parents, the childish memory he had of his mother and father had failed, only an uncle named John Dan who brought him at five years old from Zeonplay, in Nimba County, to live with Mr. Rogers. Mr. Rogers had requested the child to live with him, a debt he felt needed to be paid to the Dan.

Frank only saw his uncle two times, when he was promoted to the ninth grade and when he entered the twelfth grade. He believes Mr. Rogers and his uncle communicated somehow because it made him wonder how his uncle got information about his promotion. Frank hoped his uncle would come for his graduation since he was in Buchanan working for LAMCO, eighty-three kilometers from Monrovia. But he thought deeply that his uncle would come to see him get out of high school.

When he was promoted to the twelfth grade, he remembered his uncle saying to him using the widely spoken broken Liberian English, 'You *chief oo; our family great oo! Yor fathers, fathers, own da father, were great warriors and mighty chiefs! Our forefathers depend on you*. FraFrank's mouth drop opened. I am the poorest boy in the school, how can he sat I am great? My forefathers were great warriors and chiefs. He thought to himself.

Like Malcolm X said, *ignorance of each other is what has made unity impossible in the past*. Therefore, we need enlightenment. The settlers came to the land and chose not to know about the functionality of the natives and on the other hand, the natives never took the time to know the functionality of the settlers. Each remained within their individual enclaves, the settlers caring for their survival and writing about their heroic achievements while the natives fearing the settlers and constantly worrying about their land, not having the power to write, passed down information to succeeding generations by way of mouth. Thought to have come with the skill of writing, the settlers didn't do an all-inclusive writing on the natives until they wanted to expand into the native land. But they kept a vivid and chronological account of their being in Africa. History about both sides could have eased the tension for integration. Because both sides would have been aware of each other (though there would have been tensions that would not spilt into violence) and succeeding generations would have known and be proud of their forefathers. That's why when Frank uncle said he came from a line of great people, it sounded like a fairytale to him. Yet the lad wanted to know more about his people.

His uncle then narrated for two hours the history of his parents, grandparents, and great grandparents, and how they have led Zeonplay before the creation of the Republic of Liberia. At that time, only a few lines occurred to Frank. '*When these people came in, all were lost*,' Frank remembered his uncle sadly saying. Then underneath John Dan sad tone, the lad was frightened by the sudden change of his uncle voice to a hoarse, croaky, baritone and red, terrifying eyes, soaked in a pool of tears. Frank felt like the table shaking in line with his uncle's body movement. He felt the hate in his uncle voice. It was like his uncle had amassed this level of hatred over a long period of time. When he poured out his gut to his nephew, he needed no sympathy from him but vengeance.

"Liberia is different now, Uncle," Frank jumped in, and looked up at him.

His uncle didn't respond, but took a deep relief, wiped his tears, and said, "Shine your eyes!" He paused for a moment and said, "All I want you to know is they aren't us and we are not them. We will not mix with them until they come begging for forgiveness and pay for all our loss. . . people call you country boy," he asked Frank.

Frank nodded in affirmative and said, "But they are just joking with me. . .we all joke that way."

"It's not a joke," his uncle cried out. "I heard in America; no white man can call a black man 'nagger' without getting piece of his mouth or a blow. The word means slavery, so 'country' in Liberia means uncivilized or bush man. Don't allow anyone to call you that, it is not a joke. He is insulting you or looking down on you."

Frank was frightened by how dark his uncle had turned, sweat rolling down his face. John Dan dried his face. The expression on his uncle's face scared him to death. His eyebrows pushed up, eyes popped out, mouth spread sideway, and his uncle moved his head closer to his face.

"Do you understand," his uncle asked harshly.

Frank remembered saying yes, trembling and shaking.

"Don't learn the white people book from those civilized (Que) people; learn it for us."

Frank knew his uncle would never forget about this narrative, so he was expecting his uncle to bring up the Dans story.

"How can I hate these people when they are not all evil as my uncle believes," Franks thought. "Mr. Roger is one of them, and he treats me like his son. Although he doesn't have a child, and I don't know for what reasons, he appeared not bothered by it. Frank recorded Mr. Roger always called him his son (not biological though), and he was grateful for that and appreciated it that he was sent to the College of West Africa (CWA).

Also, at eighteen and leaving high school, Frank was thankful to Mr. Rogers for taking him as his child. Unlike other children who were brought from the interior to live with people in Monrovia and other cities around Liberia, took on new names and stayed out of schools to perform domestic tasks, Mr. Rogers refused to change Frank's name and sent him to one of the best schools in Liberia.

"Are we divided in Liberia? Is there a line," Frank thought. "If there is, why can't I see it or feel it? What did Ashmun see that I am not seeing?"

Suddenly, the loud cheers from the kitchen interrupted his thoughts. Frank looked through the window, saw the ladies dancing and smiled. He opened the paper and read through his speech, being the valedictorian.

He read the title of his speech, 'Who is a Liberian?' As he read the rest of the speech, every word meant something to him, mostly influenced by what his uncle and Ashmun told him. "Am I a chief or a person from a long line of royal family? Do I really have royalty running through me? Then how did I end up being here, common, with Mr. Rogers?"

He taught for some time and decided to ask his uncle whenever he came back. Frank sat back, and Ashmun's question came to mind, "Is oldman Monie Captain, a Liberian?"

# Chapter 7

"Why aren't children, whose parents aren't of negro descent but born in Liberia, not citizens," Frank thought. "Why parents who are naturalized citizens' children are always asked to take their parents naturalized papers to legitimize their request for legal papers?"

He thought and thought, walking in a circle in his room, trying to put the pieces together. "Caesar Gartor had said in one of his songs, he was a free-born citizen of Liberia, so he could do anything without fear. Was Caesar Gartor distinguishing himself from the others or was he trying to tell us that there were freed born of Liberia and conditional born citizens of Liberia?"

The nostalgia on his first-time meeting Ashmun was in the cafeteria. Ashmun declared that the food brought as Care food was meant for hogs and not fit for human consumption. Frank smiled and the conversation started from there. Kelvin joined their table and was introduced by Frank. Since then, they have become trios. Among the three, Ashmun was considered controversial and radical. According to him, he always sat on the floor, identifying with the many kids who had no desk to sit at in school.

A few months later, Frank met him sitting on the ground at the side of 1st Church, looking into emptiness as students were moving back and forth. He scooped up a handful of stones and began throwing them, one after the other, into the gravel pathway.

"What's up, buddy," Frank remembered saying.

Ashmun looked up at him.

Kelvin, who was tailing Frank, met the conversation. "Why is he sitting on the ground again," Kelvin asked.

"I am fine but troubled," Ashmun said, emptying the rest of the gravel on the ground. He looked at Kelvin. Kelvin smiled.

"What is troubling you, my brother," Kelvin asked.

"I was born in Liberia . . . both of my parents were born in Liberia . . . yet, I am considered white because one of my parents is pure white. Am I a Liberian? Why can't I be a Liberia?"

"What prompted this question," Franked asked, smiling.

"Answer my question first," Ashmun insisted.

"What does the constitution say?" Frank inquired further.

"The constitution denied me the right to this country," Ashmun said. "My ancestors fought for this land . . . and most died for this land, and today we have a country called Liberia because of their sacrifices. Have you not read about him? The street opposite this school, who is it dedicated to?"

Frank sat next to Ashmun and Kelvin followed.

"I am sitting by you," Frank teased, demonstrating a concept, a Liberian expression—you and I share the same story.

Kelvin took in his breath and let it out slowly.

"Well," Kelvin said, "I am in no way to speak on behalf of my people but what I do know is, we need a Liberia of inclusion.

A country living unto the true meaning of its creed, a baton of hope for the oppressed, a microcosm of the African population and an example for Africa's redemption. I see a country where a child would be freed to say, 'I am a Liberian,' despite the color of his skin or his economy status."

"I also see a Liberia where tribalism, masons, or traditional society, will not determine the outcome on an election," Frank added and smiled.

"I also see a Liberia where corrupt officials will be condemned, not praised," Kelvin said, standing. "We are the Liberia at the door to greatness and prosperity," he pointing to Frank, Ashmun and at himself.

"So true," Ashmun and Frank said together.

This discussion paved the way for the kids to label themselves The NEWGEN Initiative of Liberia. Kelvin, the son of the president of the National Bank of Liberia, a descendent of freed slaves who migrated to Liberia. They carried themselves as the brightest minds of Liberia forthrightness. The trio set up a time every Friday during recess to sell their ideas. They scheduled their first meeting the following week, and Frank was selected to initiate the discussion.

That weekend appeared gloomy, a dark gray day, painted by the continual pouring of the September rain. While students had their food, eating, Frank Dan reluctantly stood up, handshaking nervously and spoke in a cracking voice:

"Great people of the Foxes Kingdom, I salute you!"

He looked at Kelvin and Ashmun sitting at his far right. Their eyes met. Ashmun signaled him to continue.

"We are the NEWGEN Initiatives of Liberia," Frank continued, rubbing his palms together. A few students turned their attention toward him. "President John F Kennedy said, 'We are not here to curse the darkness, but to light a candle that can guide us through the darkness to a safe and sure future. For the world is changing. The old era is ending. The old ways will not do'. The problems are not all solved, and the battles are not all won, we stand today on the edge of a new frontier, a frontier of the unknown opportunities and perils, a frontier of unfulfilled hopes and threats!"

"That way we are here to ask this single complex question," Ashmun interrupted, standing. "Who is a Liberian?"

No one answered.

"I was not born when President Kennedy made those statements," Ashmun continued. "Yet, his statement speaks to me as if the president is directing us to begin the revolution . . . the revolution of consciousness!"

# *Chapter 8*

"The revolution of consciousness," someone said, from the table close to the kitchen window.

"Yes," Kelvin replied. "The revolution of consciousness! You see my brother, the mind is an amazing weapon, easily dims by lies and falsehood . . . corroded by the lack of knowledge and caged by traditions."

Kelvin walked a few steps to the center of the cafeteria.

"Any nation, whose people cannot remember the past is bound to fail several times," he continued. "Any people who will not appreciate the God-given talents its citizenry displayed in making their society a better place has no role models for its countless generations, and any people who will not hold together for the sake of their country will be control by external forces. While people with differing views see no good among themselves, and choose to remain in their sea of sameness, will continue to remain a beggar. We need an inclusive Liberia, not just a government of inclusion. And rewrite the

Liberian story; not to damned or prejudice but to know the truth and 'the truth will set us free'".

Deeply think about these questions," he continued.

Before Kelvin started to list the questions, Franks began asking the questions.

"Who is a Liberian? What qualified one a Liberian? How do the laws affect citizenships? Is dividing the country to maintain or reflect tribal boundaries and authority our problem? What is the purpose of the founding of Liberia? Why are we so afraid of one another and others? Are our laws destined to protect us or damn us? And why do we dislike the country? And promote and protect foreigners then promote and protect us? And finally, why do we always steal from ourselves?"

Then Ashmun took over from Kelvin.

"Over the years, what are the categories of people who settled on the piece of land now called Liberia?

"My people are here and in minority," Kelvin said, pointing to himself. "Frank's people have continually lived here . . . still here and in majority and at the bottom of the social ladders while Ashmun's people were once here but no longer welcome here."

"We like the way we are," a male senior student shouted, interrupting Ashmun. "Has anyone complaint to you that things aren't fine with them?"

"It's not a one-size-fit-all scenario," Ashmun answered. "This is a country with different categories of people. If I am filled and my neighbor is hungry, is that ok? If am privileged and my neighbor isn't, is that ok? If I have all the rights and my neighbors have nothing, is that ok? If I am happy and my neighbor isn't, is it that ok?"

The students couldn't answer any of Ashmun questions.

Ashmun then turned to the audience and said, "There is a new group of Liberian citizens, the children of non-negro descents borne in Liberia and children whose parents are of negro descents but from different countries) borne in Liberia. What hope do they have? What plans do we have for them? Which part of Liberia will they own? Though one of the greatest evils done to Liberia is populating people according to tribes."

"Why would you say that?" a female student shouted. "How did you think, the government who have had control over the country, will be?"

Frank stood up. But before he would speak, the student said, "The division is for administrative purposes."

Students surrounding her table cheered!

Frank waited for the cheers to die down.

"Who do you think people within the various counties show allegiance to," Frank asked. "Not to Liberia, but to the tribes and counties. People feel comfortable saying 'I am a Bassaman or Vai-man' than saying, 'I am a Liberian. I am from Lofa or Grand Kru,' instead of saying, 'I am from the Southeast or northern region'. Before the Republic of Liberia, these people Lived here side by side. How do you think they survived to this day? They look at themselves as kins and not tribes."

"I still believed people don't get it . . . that they belong to Liberia," Kelvin said.

Frank sat and said, "This demarcation was for control, divide, and rule . . . and it allowed tribes to retreat into their little corners. . . suppressed, oppositions crushed, and humiliated by Monrovia. Tribal lines were the only safe havens; great men who rose up to fight the system were bribed and/or hung publicly to demonstrate Monrovia's meanness."

Everyone stopped eating, all eyes fixed on the three young men.

"Take for example," Ashmun stated, "Kru Town, Bassa Community, Buzi Quarter, etc . . . do you know why they were established?"

Nobody answered but stared at one another.

"To control the influx into Monrovia and how tribal people moved or lived in the city," Ashmun responded. "There were the Hut Tax and the pawn systems and . . . ."

"You aren't a Liberian, despite being born in the country. We love how we are," Tiny Mayors said, pointing at Ashmun. Tiny was the head of the school cheer team.

Ashmun smiled, turned to Frank, and winked.

Frank walked slowly towards the table Tiny was seated at and stopped.

"My dear Tiny," Frank said, "what is the street's name opposite our school?"

"Ashmun Street," Tiny replied.

"And if I may ask, who was Jehudi Ashmun according to Liberian History?"

Tiny froze, speechless.

"That fellow," Frank pointed at Ashmun. "He is a descendant of Jehudi Ashmun who fought to keep the colony called Liberia alive. He lost his wife on this soil, the very place where we are standing. You denied him and his descendent citizenship but honored him with a street . . . what an irony."

"On the issue honoring Ashmun," Kelvin cut in. "Recess is almost over; I want to say this, then Ashmun or Frank can close the discussion. My people were very afraid, and their fear got us to this place."

Everyone looked stunted.

"Why didn't we honor any native," Kelvin continued. "Because they fought against us for their land, or we never considered them citizens of Liberia? If we cannot consider those who fought with us and used their money and resources to establish this country to become citizens, how about those who fought against us? About the US, we honored that country that doesn't care about us and has never admitted they colonized us with everything, including our life and our direction. The US can never love us because we are black, and we mean nothing to them."

"So true brother," someone yelled from the audience.

"As cancerous as the issue of race is," Kelvin continued. "When it takes hold of you, it eats away the good embedded in anyone. Why couldn't the United States, for once, do a good thing for a group of people who labored for their country for those extended periods of time? Like it did for the Israeli, as it did for the Taiwanese, as it did for the Philippians and other places where American goodwill is displayed."

This is why we need to rethink the direction of our country," Ashmun added. "Do we want to continue living in a 'Cow Pupu' Country? Where we are greatly divided, hate prevalence, envy, and intolerance our daily tonic . . . poverty that has breed dishonesty guiding our decisions, morality kicked out, and our role models bad judgement and has continually elevated strangers to 'hide us from washing our dirty clothes' from the rest of the world," He concluded in time for the recess bell.

Frank still remembered that one fateful day, and the aftermath. It was in late September, though it was mid-December, it was just yesterday when the assistant principal put an end to what Frank thought would have been the energizer to revive Liberia.

Liberia and the older generation, a piece of the puzzle of wisdom. Since the era of Liberia's enlightenment, their wisdoms of Hut Tax, Open Door Policy, So-say-one, so-says-all, they vs us, membership in the brotherhood of secrecy, political and social correctness, selfishness, nepotism, dishonesty, congoes-settlers-natives nonsense, religious doormats, etc., has provided no pathways for growth and development. They have proven to be the values passed down to the present generation to take Liberia forward. It's shameless to say Liberia will drown in this sea of sameness. It would be a disservice to say Liberia has no 'good souls.' There are many good people and role models, but in a country where the few 'rotten apples' make sure to yank power or are in positions of trust, one rethinks an alternative to the democratic process. These few groups of people copied these mean strategies from succeeding generations to perpetuate their grip on the country. They are or have clinked to the 'forces that drive' Liberia and hammering every effort to kick (through every means) their opponents out, blooming the ways for foreigners to be richer than the people and blocked and or will frustrate anyone who bypass their dragnet. But remember, the rest of the puzzle! What has happened to it? They need to take control of the country and demand the government to recognize their positions. And correct the notions that the 'young minds' only offer childish wisdoms and rethink the cultural that forbit young people from questioning or arguing with older folks.

It has long been said, *'the younger generation needs to sit on the old mat to plait their way forward'*. What do the few influential and powerful 'old mat' have to offer? It is nothing but a dangerous cultural trend that the younger generation has no wisdom. So, Frank believes the NewGen would have been the beginning of discussing Liberia into the future. But labeling the discussion—matters contrary to the principles of Liberia's foundation—was a symptom of the cancer of fears of reprisal and attitude of numbness that engulfed Liberia for so long. But he and the rest of the NewGen had a successful school year. Ashmun and Kelvin had been accepted to travel abroad to further their studies. Thanks to bilateral scholarships spread across various government ministries and agencies. Frank had one only hope, the University of Liberia.

Just like many before him, Frank finds himself in a whirlwind of uncertainty. He was smart, full of energy, and hopeful, but he could not understand why he was below that opportunity. Like a black man born and living in the United States, he had that conceptualized idea of being a citizen of Liberia. And living in the misconception that he was someway, somehow a citizen of the US and protected by the United States. Maybe he was fooled by what he heard and saw: the flag, the pledge, the forms and structure of government, the accents of the people around him, the music, the foods, cultures, the names of places, and many more.

The United States is a mirage. Frank sighed. A land founded on the belief that all men are created equal is struggling with the true nature of its creed. They always strive to interpret the phrase '*all persons are created equal*'. There are those who believe to be true Americans versus Immigrants and there are white Americans versus black Americans, and the true owners of the land placed in the dark and made powerless, to be forgotten. A mistake that is now being corrected.

Frank believes this is the same strategy the founding fathers implemented in Liberia. The strategy of keeping the original owners of the land now called Liberia in the dark, depraved, and forgotten. Unlike the US, the founding fathers uprooted the structure, paused the people's history, and left them in a state of oblivion like a snake without a head. Like the US, the founding fathers wanted their kind to be heard, to shine, and to continue their hegemony. He believes this was the biggest mistake made during the building of the foundations of Liberia. For the founding fathers to anticipate controlling a landmass full of people from different tribal backgrounds and leaving them without their individual leadership. But a false hope of unification under a Monrovia leadership.

"I wished the tribes were controlled through their kings/ chiefs," he thought. "There would have been a sense of control and discipline, and the people would have had a say in exploiting their God-given natural resources.'

But as so-called investors entered Liberia, everything surrounding his investments is known in Monrovia, driven by Monrovia, fueled by Monrovia, securitized by Monrovia, and controlled by Monrovia. Leaving the people in those dirt-poor regions at the mercy of the so-called investors. They exploited the land, exploited the people and children, separated families, destroyed traditional shrines, killed people, and whipped oppositions under the watchful eyes of Monrovia. Monrovia is comfortable, has pipe borne water, has electricity, better health system, and stable life. No worries about those outside of Monrovia, living in riches but poor, lacking the know-how to transform their environment, their lives and wellness. The irony of life in Monrovia, surprises Frank. Monrovia is a replica of a quicksand, absorbing the best of bests, the innocents, the blinds and the enlightened into the vortex of a corrupt and evil system. Most people from the interiors of Liberia sent their children to Monrovia to get a Western education and hoped those children, upon graduation, would help get them out of their misery. But once the children acquired the western education, they abandoned their people, will demonize, and denigrate them, or remained in Monrovia to escape the claws of the witches and wizards.

Frank peeped through the window, in response to a loud roar. A lady brought in a cartoon of Stockton Gin from Leroy Francis' Factory. Mr. Francis had his factory on Jamacia Road. It was rumored that he distilled and supplied the finest Liberia gin to the people in the slums of Monrovia.

Monrovia is a two-face community, running from Mamba Point to the Atlantic Ocean, to the Du Rivers, down to the City Hall of Monrovia, is the workstations and homes to the rich and powerful of Liberia while Bushord Island and Sinkor to the rest of Liberia is home to the poor and depraved. These two halves equal Liberia. A country founded to repatriate freed US slaves to Africa. With the impression that those freed slaves would have better chances for freedom and prosperity in the land of their ancestors. So, the settlers and those allowed them settled are called Liberian citizens.

"Citizens?" Frank breathed out the word. "Am I really a citizen of Liberia?" he asked himself. He had heard several versions of the citizens' story narrated from people's experiences. "Some people told their stories of being contesting with a foreigner for contracts while others told their stories interacting with other Liberia or from different point of views. All the stories painted one story: foreigners are privileged than Liberian citizens.

# Chapter 9

Frank gained consciousness and went over his speech rehearsing aloud. The United States, yes, the US and Liberia relationships kept clouding his mind. He knew the United States didn't care about Liberia, but Liberians brainwashed to believe in the United States. The United States foreign policy towards Liberia changes to an extend (and overtime) diminishes to its succeeding generations as a 'causal relationship' and negating any claims of neglect and destruction on the part of the US.

Frank believed the United States should have accepted responsibilities, for its citizens who were deployed on the continent of Africa. The US should have told the truth that it mandated its citizens to Christianized and civilized the dark continent. A dark continent? Christening Africa sounds like a fallacy because Christianity reached Africa before there was a place called the United States. But like the rest of the world, Africa is caught between the race for supremacy and dominance between Islam and Christianity. So, the US sent its citizens to colonize the people of Africa and exactly they did. They changed the form of government accustomed to the inhabitants; they changed the names of the land; they ushered in their form of communication and their dress codes; they introduced their foods, music, arts, and cultures, and just everything, the United States. But what did the US do for its citizens on the continent of Africa? Unlike the US, Great Britain accepted that it colonized the Gold Coast, Sierra Leone, etc., and France colonized Senegal and Ivory Coast, amongst others. Looking at the laws of the United States, no damn organization has the power to colonize a piece of land.

It is crystal clear this declaration won't change anything, but let the truth be told. The American Colonization Societies (ACS) were surrogate of the United States government. To this day, the US ignored, lied, and refused to take responsibility. Was it because of the color of their skin? What if they were white? I believe the US would have been happy to claim the land. But they were the United States slaves, and black.

Not just black, but the United States blacks, uneducated, freed, but in chains. Yes, uneducated about themselves! Uneducated to the land they occupied. Uneducated to the people who allowed them to settle in! Uneducated to the environment, biodiversity, and environs! Yes, still uneducated to the form of government given them, and uneducated to the working therein! Uneducated in the principles of governance! Uneducated in the management of resources and accounting for it! Uneducated to self-disciplines, and the value that comes with knowing oneself! Uneducated to principles of physics and chemistry and, engineering! But educated to the teaching of the gospel reinforced by white missionaries who grew up hating black people or uneducated to the composition of humanity.

Oh, what did the US do, provided the opportunities for its missionaries to enlighten and or understand black people in Africa as opposed to understanding them in the US where more enlightenment, education and understanding of black people necessary for the 'real composition' of the USA.

In Africa, the US missionaries learned that black people in Africa are humans, nothing more, nothing less. Though, they succeeded in reprogramming the young ones to disperse his people and cultures, reducing the traditional dispenser of justice to evil called the 'devil' and their dwelling place, 'devil bush'. They reprogramed the young people to believe their people are barbarians and rejected by God, and their names connote evils. They made sure to teach that God has abandoned black people and are heading for hell fire. Names that were difficult to pronounce or spell (never took the time to learn it) were replaced with western names.

So, they taught black people that the only way out is to accept the religion of the pure, (a twisted version of Christianity), taking on a new identity name.

Mankind search for God can be moderate and extreme. He will destroy others in the name of God or control other for His names' sake. Since Cain and Abel, mankind had been competing or revenging for God. A task that not theirs, but men professed to have heard God's instructions, to destroy or control others into submission. A foolish exertion. As it was on the Grain Coast, the strategy was organized, universal and executed differently according to regions.

For the US, what was the plan? Not to be held liable for sending portion of its negroes' citizens away, he allowed his organizations to take charge. And like Pilate, he watched from a distance and supported the organizations.

Liberia established through racial prejudice; land gotten through trickery; built on lies and division, and people caged and numbed, Killed, and reprogramed to follow order and discard their 'Africaness'. While they preached love, their actions were different.

Since they preached Love, Liberia needs to harness that resilient force to crafting a new Liberia for all. A new Liberia that will give more power to the people and if anyone who wants to do business will go directly to the people, not to the politicians in Monrovia.

The land in Liberia most often referred to as property of a tribal people, but what really give them the power to show that that asset truly theirs?

Love will urge us to pursue a path for national awareness on *who is a Liberian and the future of Liberia*' seeing in the eyes of the present generation.

Therefore, every journey has a beginning. The Liberia's journey (from the beginning to the present) has glitches we must first acknowledged: in the beginning people died, people were cheated, lied to, frustrated, neglected, torn apart, and some much more. Well, I believe it started with the taking over of the tribal shrines belonging to the Bassa People, which it was desecrated for the building of a church, where Liberia's Declaration of Independence was signed, the double-dealing and denial of the United States of colonizing Liberia. I wonder what was Jehudi Ashmun doing in the new colony? Who was he working for? What did Robert F, Stockton do to the tribal chief at Cape Mesurado? Who killed Governor Josiah F. Finley? How many white people died during the founding of Liberia? Why was Settra Kroo envied? Why do we celebrate Joseph J Roberts and others when (in facts) they didn't write the declaration of independence, the first constitution and all other proclamations for Liberia? Without giving their input on how they wanted the country to be governed or the country stratified, they just accepted the document and executed it.

No, they look at it! How do I know, they altered it to not allow their slave masters and their children (though several died in making Liberia) who would want to be a part of this country? What more needed to be told? The ritualistic killing! How many persons needed to be killed for power? How many will be left to raise up Liberia? Do members of the disbanded Leopold Society still hire to get rid of political opponents? Everything is just going in a circle. Those people are all old and most are gone, but the killing continue. Is there a new breed of killers? Was this art of killing passed on or a work of the disbanded rebel forces? Maybe we need to investigate how the interactions of the various commissioners in the counties and the government in Monrovia. Should Firestone pay reparation to those who were driven from their ancestor? Should they be made to pay for the destruction of the sacred forests?

We also need to investigate Yarkpwolo versus the Government in Firestone. We need to search to see why and how those things happened. For the truth to be told! Since we now know the world is no more policed by a lone-avatar of force, the US, we Liberians (Liberia) need to rethink our strategies for global (political and economic) engagements for the ultimate growth and survival of our people.

# Chapter 10

Frank pondered and took one last look at the page, a paragraph popped up: 'in the pursuit of freedom everyone is a brother; later, power will draw a line and the weaklings will have to submit. The rods will ignite fears, then fear will lead the search for enlighten and there will be revolution. In the real-world cycle'. Frank smiled after reading through, took a final look in the mirror, his black gown gives elegance to the white shirt and black tie. He repositioned his mortar board, made a simpering smile, and went out to where the ladies were cooking.

Frank was greeted by jubilant cheers; the ladies took out the pieces of lappas surrounding the main garment and spread them on the floor for him to walk on. They circled him, singing and dancing in the Kru and Bassa languages. Mr. Rogers was believed to be from the Bassa and Kru ethnic groups, and the ladies were his relatives who had volunteered to prepare the food for the celebration of Frank Dan from high school.

One of the ladies led him to the porch and ushered into a chair that had a lappa covering.

"Let me bring small palm butter rice for you to eat before going," the lady said and went to the kitchen.

She returned a few minutes later with the food.

Frank thanked the lady and began eating spoonsful of the delicious meal. He put down the bowl when he saw Mr. Rogers arrive in a rental taxi. The driver unloaded bags of ice from the taxi and took them to the ladies in the kitchen.

"Your son is ready . . . he is on the porch," Mr. Roger's cousin said to him. "Can I bring you some food to eat before leaving for the program?"

"No Gbalie, we are almost late for the ceremony," he said and walked to where Frank was sitting.

"Are you ready, son?"

"Yes."

"You are just like your mother," Mr. Rogers said, staring at Frank. "Your father's 'pop' eyes and his strife for excellence endowed with leadership and resilience, are your glory."

"You knew my parents?" Frank asked.

Mr. Rogers smiled and said, "Let's talk about this another time, Son. You are a Dan, and the Dan has a unique and long history in northern Liberia. Let's go to the car."

They walked to the Honda; Frank sat in the back seat while Mr. Rogers took the passenger seat in the front. The driver started the ignition and pulled away, driving to Monrovia.

Mr. Rogers turned to Frank and said, "I know your family history . . . I saw your grandfather. Your father and I were friends in Nimba."

Frank grew up not knowing his biological parents. According to information he heard from people, his father was a headman for Lamco in Yekepa, Nimba County. But both parents disappeared without trace, leaving him a lone soul to be cared for by Mr. Rogers. As a next-door neighbor to John Dan and his wife Sankay, in Area E, working as an assistant to John, Mr. Rogers's home was opened to the Dans. They were all best friends, playing checkers, cards, and soccer together. But then John and Sankay went for a walk on the road that led to the mountains and never returned, creating a two-day search. The police and Plant Protection Forces used their sophistication but yielded no results. All eyes were turned on Mr. Rogers, who people believed wanted John's position, so he killed or used juju to get rid of him and his wife.

John Dan was a descendant of Gonganue Dan, the ousted Town Chief, during the Republic of Liberia's expansion into the interior of Liberia. His father was Gaye, the sixth generation of the Dan. John still remembered the story about what happened to the remaining family members of the Dan. The Liberian Frontier Force (LFF) took his forefathers and group of men from the town known as 'Government Bones' and taken to the coast to clear the piece of land to host the Firestone Rubber Plantation.

It is still unclear how Firestone got that land and how it paid one cent per acre for ninety-nine years. Did Firestone pay the wrong tenants, or the legal tenants were (a repeat of history) put at gunpoint to provide the parcel of land for its operations? Some will argue that the land was closer to the base for the United States military. But how did the US military get the land? Who were the principal occupants? Where did they go? Were they relocated with benefits? Some of those people lived in those places for a very long time, and to be pushed away or relocated, required new survival skills. So, what is a government that removes its people from their legal land without compensation? The Government of Liberia could not pay its employees nor provide basic social services for those within its enclaves but stood with those who came to exploit its citizens. It never advocated for the just benefits of its other citizens but collected all the royalties for the support and comfort of its other citizens in Monrovia. While their lives were improving, those outside Monrovia (with the resources) were worsening.

Clearly, the Government of Liberia could still not exert complete control over the landmass of the Grain Coast. It couldn't protect families from being separated during the land grabbing initiated by France and Great Britain or keep down local military insurrections. These people outside of Monrovia fought the French and Britain fought for their survival, their land, and their families. The government couldn't help them because it didn't believe in their strength though their skills in warfare were clearly displayed through a wall built in Yeala near ZorZor. A culture that started and still prevalent, cutting across the entire country, nobody trust the ability of his countrymen like they would lay down their lives for the foreigners. And preferred having anything (substandard) over what has produced in the country.

All the Republic of Liberia did was cried to the United States (its stepfather). What good is a government that can't recognize the strength and determination of his people? What good is a government who's willing to squeeze its people to their death to better its cronies, its kinds, and foreigners?

Few natives saw this injustice, including Chief Gonganue and the Klao Chiefs, but they too were branded as troublemakers and hung. It still didn't change anything. People are still branded as troublemakers and most of the time hanged, murdered, or go missing if they spoke against injustices and request equal access to the wealth of the country. This new way of attaining power instills fear and silence in an age-old tradition of dominance and inferiority complex in a patriarchal society. This culture created a new generation of people with the psychic of servants, who suppressed their brilliance and walked in insecurity. So, when someone wants to be different, he's targeted. This was the fate of Gonganue and others, leaving their family scattered and serving as government bones.

*Government Bones* is a phrase coined by the locals for those who were forced to offer their service to the government of Liberia. Government Bones were made to clear high bushes to roads, clear parcels of land for what were called government farms, and transport officials and visitors in hammocks.

So, the government called those people *'troublemakers'* and wanted to send them to a faraway place. The men were rounded up, banded by ropes (as if during the time of slavery) and taken on a long journey. Few survived while others died along the route. Those who tried to escape, were gunned down or hung, and their bodies displayed to prevent would-be escapees. Women and children were left alone; wives without husbands and children without fathers.

# Chapter 11

In the early 1930s, Gaye married a mano girl, Yah. Yah was also Government Bones. She was a 'pawn' to covered up the money her parents owed a soldier. Their union produced two sons, Alfred and Timothy. Prior to meeting Yah, Gaye had been converted to Christianity by a minister from Monrovia. He was running a local church in his community and referred to as Pastor Gaye. He didn't continue carrying his surname.

Every culture is unique, and there's something that distinguishes one culture from another. This thing that cut across the culture of the people living on the piece of land prior to the creation of Liberia is the use of the surname. Everybody was known by his given name and the name of one's father was only mentioned when they wanted to distinguish a person during a conversation. For example, if someone was having a conversation with another and he asked:

"*Do you know Kerkula?*" For the other person who's in doubt and doesn't know which Kerkula was being referred to, the speaker will then clarify this way: "*Kerkula, Kollie's son?*" The culture of identifying a person by his given name was handed down through the ages.

Mr. Rogers had to resign, contacted John's brother in Buchanan, and ended up taking care of the child. He came back to Monrovia and got a job with the government. Frank began his primary school at Isaac Davis School. The lad was bright; Mr. Roger noticed that in him and found a tutor for him.

Upon graduation from the Isaac Davis School, Frank got a scholarship to the College of West Africa (CWA). At CWA, Frank befriended Kelvin Benson, son of the National Bank Governor. Kelvin, who already had a best friend, Montgomery Ashmun, got close to Frank after a Science Project in the eleventh Grade. Montgomery, Frank, and Kelvin called themselves the Trio. The Trio organized study sessions to help students who were too slow to learn math, physics, and chemistry. That's how the Trio lead the school; Montgomery was the school president, Kelvin, the vice President, and Frank, Secretary and Valedictorian.

Montgomery, born in Upper Buchanan, Liberia, along the route to the historic Edina community. The family house is next to Mother Dukuly's institute for girls. He started his elementary and junior high school at Clever High School. At Clever, he was called the 'white boy' in a black skin. He spoke the Bassa language fluently and conversed in the Liberian English without problems.

His surname is synonymous to the founding of Liberia. It is known among the Bassa people that Montgomery is a descendent of Jehudi Ashmun, the man who gave his life fighting to keep the colony now called Liberia, standing. Controversial as his critic referred to him, who didn't believe in the equality of blacks and whites, he wanted a United States empire in Africa.

After his death in 1828, the name Ashmun disappeared from the Liberian landscape until after ninety-nine years, when a descendent of Jehudi Ashmun came to Liberia in the early 1920s for a fixability study on the construction of a port at Bushord Island.

Montgomery Ashmun, the lad's great-great grandfather (whom he's named after) migrated to Liberia in the 20s as a civil engineer to research the ocean to find a land place for the Firestone establishment and possible construction of a port of entry. In 1948, he was part of the army engineering team which built an artificial harbor with two breakwaters on Bushord Island, near Monrovia. He decided to live in Monrovia. While living in Liberia, Montgomery usually traveled to the United States for his annual medical check-up. When asked why he was living in a country with no modern hospital and fewer doctors, he would say "I feel entitled to that country." He would add further, "My forefathers fought for that country. My forefather spent his life in stabilizing that country, and my forefather is the reason why there is a country called Liberia."

# Chapter 12

Montgomery met a British research nurse and they got married. They stayed in Monrovia, and had his grandfather, Alban Ashmun, who later worked at the Free Port of Monrovia as an engineer. Alban met Catharine Garrett of New York. Catharine was in Liberia as a Peace Corp Volunteer. This union produced Timothy Ashmun, commonly called Tim. Tim was assigned as Deputy Port Manager for Operation at the port of Buchanan. Tim met Marpue Horace in Buchanan and they got married and had Montgomery. Marpue was mixed, mother, Lebanese, and father, Bassa. A union is uncommon in Liberia. The males from different cultures were opportune to marry Liberian women and not the opposite. A girl who wanted to be different was always on the next plane. Thus, restricting her freedom to choose her life partner.

Liberia was established as a haven for those who fled prosecution. Though created on an idea, the Liberian Dream still has never been realized. During the administration of President William V.S. Tubman, a flicker of freedom, opportunity, liberty, and good life sprung in this divided nation with false hope. The era was ripe for the plunder of resources, but the managers and laws they crafted favored the strangers. The world raced to Liberia for the resources, each coming with its culture and traditions. Marpue's great-grandfather came from a cultural background where finding a suitor was the father's prerogative. A complete opposite of the modern Liberian Dream. The Liberian Dream is defined as a culture created to defy traditions and alter religion. A culture in which one is free to do whatever he/she wants to do and can do whatever he/she wants to do or free to marry whom he/she chooses.

Marpue's great-grandfather, a young man who migrated to Liberia in the early 20s. He opened a department store down Water Street, Monrovia, near the Ferry Station. The Ferry Station was the regulatory point for the ferry going back and forth on the Mesurado River transporting passengers to Bushord Island and Monrovia, and verse versa.

In the early 60s, her grandfather moved to Buchanan and opened a store at the St. John River crossing point. When he passed away, his son, Farhat, took over the store and he married Soraya, a bride brought in from Bruit by his uncle. This union produced two boys (Assi and Elie) and a girl (Alaa).

The Trios saw and lived in a flawless Liberia, and their differing socio-economic conditions were no spooky monster. As for Frank, his past was unknown to him. His story hung on oral history. A method of storing information is susceptible to inaccuracy as it would be passed down from one generation to another by way of mouth. Frank didn't know he had royal blood, a Dan, and that his great-great-great-grandfather was one of the mighty chiefs on the Grain Coast. He didn't know that prior to the execution of his great-great-great-grandfather, he visited several chiefs, including Chief Sua Coco and the successor of Chief Boso, in their native countries to resist the complete control of the native countries by the Republic of Liberia. He could not find it in any history books of Liberia that Chief Dan told those chiefs that once Liberia couldn't protect the native countries (people, land, cultures, and secured forests) from expansions of Great Britain and France, Liberia was incapacitated to handle the affairs of the native countries. He wanted the native countries to govern themselves.

Nations all over the world look to the one who they believe is capable of leading and protecting their ideas and beliefs. Some find this person amongst their populations while others hold onto the ones who redeemed them from calamity. And when this person is found, the people surrender and follow him. Therefore, on the Grain Coast, the chiefs had a special place in the mind of their people, they saw the chief as their father, looked to him as their leader, the caretaker of the land, their individual families, their traditions, and cultures. He stood as their pride and dignity, their symbol and protector of the land. He has been and is a representative of their gods, interacting with the Zoes and all spiritual heads, and accountable to only the grand wizard and elders. Anyone who wanted land to farm or build a house went to him and never to anyone else. Strangers were his responsibility, and the safety of people from other tribes who settled in his countries was his duty.

But histories of the native population in Liberia had not been given complete coverage. Their day-to-day life had not been explained; their unique cultures, their resilience in keeping their various native country together and the understanding, and not even the greatest of kings (chiefs) who led their people against invaders, the battles they won, the greatest courage they exhibited against the British, French, and the Republic of Liberia, land grabbed were canceled. A carefully crafted plan to erase the long-standing traditions and history of a group of people cannot be understood. Some people believed it was the Americo-Liberian's way of payback for being sold into slavery, while others think the Americo-Liberian just didn't care. The majority think it was the Americo-Liberian way of keeping the natives in the dark (unaware of their strength and their history) to avoid rebellion.

All they did was use their historians to write nonfictional stories that showed the natives as victims, cruel, backward, and lacking sound judgment until they came in. The historians wrote about how they were sold into slavery, how Bob Gray sold his land for 'smoke fish', how those from Nimba ate human being, and all the negativities.

Why have they not written the positives, how the natives had a system of governments that were unique, a culture that were astonishing, how the native towns were cleaned, how they allowed strangers to travel throughout their countries without a visa, how they traded with people from other countries. Not even the negatives of concerns, how several Kru chiefs were hung because they opposed the Republic of Liberia, how the settlers cut down the major shrine belonging to the Mamba People, (built a church on the land) and signed the declaration of independence, not even mentioned how the natives taught the settlers to survive and farmed the mosquitoes infested land, left out the voices of those who called for integration, never talked about how natives were cheated with the idea of a land sale, a culture that foreign to them, about the Hut Tax and the Pawn system, the period the natives were not citizens of Liberia, and how they were ill-treated in the hands of the settlers, about how the settlers completely destroyed a way of life of a particular people. Historians never mentioned in totality the recaptured slaves, not even a catalog of their existence and of those from the Caribbeans, their contribution and uniqueness. They forgot even those who fled from other parts of Africa due to injustice, war, and hardship and made it to Liberia for greener pastures. These are narratives that are left out of Liberia's story. It is important to the unification, growth, and development of the country. It is proven (though not scientifically) that fear, jealousy, striving for material wealth and influence, tribalism, nepotism, intolerance, and hatred, amongst others, are the aftereffects of the ways the country has been stratified for control and check. And exacerbated by the creation of the commissioners, Tubman's Public Relation Policy, angered from the Hut Tax and Pawn system, and the Monrovia elites versus the rest of the country.

Consistence with the overall growth and development of the country, is the understanding that a republic is different from a democracy, and all Liberians be aware of the difference. Is Liberia a republic, a democracy, or a hybrid? Are the issues of land reflecting the present reality? Each tribal county has a chief (serve by term) who is the chief administrator of that tribal land.

Is citizenship clear to everyone? Liberia is a combination of various groups of people who arrived at different periods. Who then is a Liberian, needs to be clarified, incorporating everyone into a homogenous unit, and amended by the constitution? Laws (crafted) that target only Liberians and not foreigners, and dawn anyone has stolen from the country.

Is the working of the three branches of government clearly explained? How can we prevent one powerful branch from interfering with the workings of the other (one or) two branches without reprisals? How do the people challenge an autocratic regime without waiting for elections? How do we give authority to chiefs so they can exercise their control without fear of reprisal from superintend, lawmakers, and or the president?

We must rethink Liberia and define the kind of Liberia we want for ourselves and the next generations of Liberians. We are special; the old ways have not helped us. I am sincerely sure that these actions will propel Liberia into a single, united but diversified community.

Brenda Cooper stepped out of the house, tastefully dressed in one of the fashionable styled dresses in town. The sweetness of the morning breeze greeted and refreshed her entire body.

Now she felt relaxed and realized she has been left alone to walk from her fifth street residence to Tubman Blvd to get a taxi to Town for training computer software. This six-month training course filled the void Brenda felt in sitting at home after graduating from B.W Harris High School. B.W. Harris, a church-run school that incorporated children from every spare of life.

Within a land mass equivalent to seventy-five squire miles, hosting the seats of government and commercial activities, Monrovia is the backbone of Liberia. Just as Mamba Point attracts all diplomatic missions and hotels, so is Capitol Hill, the helm of powers and education. Central Monrovia incorporates the cinemas, discos, restaurants, and the Palm Grove cemetery, Post Stockage (prison), Antoinette Tubman Sport stadium, Waterside Market, the Barclay Training Center, and West Point.

From the sky, Monrovia is a beauty to adore; but down below, a haven for the haves and the have-nots. Therefore, the communities within Monrovia are a mixture of residentials and commercial activities.

Each day, like a flock of sheep, everyone went to Monrovia (Town) in the morning and exited during the evening time. This morning and evening routine makes 'Town' a joyous place in the day and a ghostly place at night. Except for the few residents who struggle to keep the night spirit lighted. Town, a common name known among the population of Monrovia, is used in daily discussions.

Brenda's father, Gerald Cooper, traveled to the Robert International Airport (RIA) to pick up his sister, Joyce, who was returning from Japan. Joyce's husband was the head of the government of Liberia's diplomatic mission to Seoul and Tokyo.

As she stood by the road awaiting a taxi, she still heard her father's words: "stay out of the way of bad boy and girl. Do you understand?".

When Brenda nodded, he asked, "You heard me?" in a blistering voice.

"I heard you Daddy," Brenda answered.

She knew her father and had endured those tones of voice since age six. Though she knew he loved her and was protecting her, he hadn't realized that she was eighteen, legally an adult.

By the law of Liberia, anyone who reaches the age of eighteen is an adult. Parents have ignored those laws and allowed their children to stay overtime. Most parents allowed their children to stay and finish college, while others allowed them out once they were ready to marry. Even if they are married, some parents would appreciate their children living with their spouse in the home. Since she was not an adult enough to live on her own, Brenda chose to remain under her parents' roof and go to college. If a suitor came by, she preferred to be taken out of her parent's home. A respectable and perceived orderly transitional arrangement a girl would wish for.

# Chapter 13

Liberians attitude towards marriage dangled in two philosophies, indigenous and western. Both were understandably accurate according to their settings and institutionalization. The Indigenous ideal modes of marriage dictated by individual tribal procedure while the western synonymous to the settler's idea of marriage they learned from the western world. Though separate in preceding but identical in ways, parents scouted for partners for their children. Brenda would wish for the Western since she is a descendant of the settlers (Americo-Liberian).

According to the story, on November 3, 1851, her great-great-great-grandparents sailed from Baltimore on the Morgan Dix to Liberia. Brenda was the twelve generation of the Coopers. Like her grandparents, her father was Secretary of the Department of Commerce, Industry, and Transportation (Ministry of Commerce).

Endowed with a quiet and gentle spirit and beauty of the 'golden plum', a height of 5'6', and a smile that melts an angry soul, Brenda carried herself with pride and dignity. She always embraced life with its natural scenery. That was why she always helped her mother, MaRose Cooper, with the garden of roses. When the roses blossomed, she would smile at the garden of multiple natural-colored roses and be delighted by the sweet fragrance that greeted her. To her their positions never matter; together, they made the yard a beauty to adore.

Mr. Cooper exemplified modesty and tolerance, a father of four boys and a daughter, and had lots of natives who lived under his roof to be educated. One day, Brenda remembered her father saying to one of the native boys who chose to use the Cooper name instead of his native name in school, 'Remember,' her father said to the boy. 'There will come a time when your parents' name will be important as my name.'

Brenda loved her father for his concern for other people, but nobody messes with his daughter. He was happy that she was left alone to flag down a taxi to town for her post high school computer training. She still couldn't remember the last time she rode a taxi. Brenda looked left and right on the four-lane road; no vehicle was traveling toward the first two lanes. She crossed and stood on the double bold yellow lines separating the road. Two vehicles sped past, and she quickly ran to the other side of the street. She stood before the building hosting the Ministry of Youth and Sport.

Brenda was aware that crossing Tubman Boulevard required one to be attentive. It was a common place for accidents. A 40 MPH road was usually taken advantage of by all the drivers. The speed sign was broken down, and the city government felt wary of putting up another one. With no speed limit sign, drivers could zoom up to 60 or 75 MPH.

Kelvin Benson's girlfriend, Caroline Thomas, and buddy Frank Dan were driving from Paynesville to Town in a BMW.

Kelvin was driving, Caroline was seated in the passenger seat in the front, and Frank was in the back seat. They were going to shop for the July 26th celebration.

"Do you know that Ashmun went to college in the United States?" Frank interrupted, attempting to shift Kelvin from arguing with Caroline. Caroline was concerned and disliked the way Kelvin was speeding on Tubman Boulevard. More especially when he nearly hit a man who was running across the road. In no time they had passed the USAID compound on 9th Street.

"Yes, he got a scholarship from Cornell University,'" Kelvin replied, keeping his eyes on the road.

Kelvin passed the Greenland Supermarket with light speed.

"Kelvin stopped!" Frank yelled.

Kelvin pressed the brake hard.

"Please give that girl a ride," Frank asked.

Kelvin reversed and stopped directly in front of Brenda.

"Excuse me beautiful," Frank stuck his head out the window, looking at Brenda. "My name is Frank Dan. Can we give you a ride to Town?"

Brenda looked up at the sky, then at Frank.

"Getting a taxi this time is difficult," Frank added.

"Why don't you join us," Caroline suggested. "We are all young people."

Brenda smiled and reluctantly joined Frank in the back seat. She introduced herself. Kelvin and Caroline introduced themselves respectively.

"A beautiful name and smile," Frank said. 'You are as 'fresh and pretty' as Musu Page, Miss. Liberia. Do you know you can win that crown?"

"Sorry Frank," Brenda said. "I'm the shy type and don't like being advertised."

"Are you allowed visitors?" Frank asked.

"No, especially strangers . . . my father doesn't allow strangers."

Frank sighed, showing disappointment.

"Since we are getting to know each other, I don't think we are strangers anymore," Frank insisted.

"No," Brenda said, moving her head from side to side. "Not even a girl can visit me at my house."

"Does that mean after today I will never see you again?"

"I hope not," Brenda replied.

"Brenda, what part of town are you stopping at," Kelvin asked.

"Randall Street . . . near the Ministry of Planning."

Kelvin looked in the rearview mirror and saw Frank staring at Brenda. "Are you ok, Frank?" he asked.

Before Frank made an answer, Kelvin said, "Brenda, why don't you go with us shopping for the 26th celebration?"

Brenda looked at Kelvin. What does he want? She thought.

"How long your class last for?" Kelvin asked.

"Forty-five minutes. Why?"

"I like your conversation," Frank said. "Besides, we would like to get to know you."

"Yes, we need to read your book," Frank joked. "Please say 'yes'."

After dropping Brenda off at the computer school, Frank suggested they drive around town and wait for her.

"Seriously!" Caroline and Kelvin said together.

A burst of lighters followed.

"You just met this girl and you're craving after her," Caroline said. "Be careful ooo. . . to love someone is a process, and there is no magic wane."

Frank stopped smiling.

"Caroline, if Frank is falling for her, it's a good thing. There are many ways to fall in love, but the hard part is waiting, not knowing if the girl will agree."

Everybody laughed.

"Kelvin, we need to hurry up and go to get Brenda because I can't wait another second without seeing her," Frank said.

Caroline stared at him shaking her head. "You have to be careful, Frank," she added.

They picked up Brenda and drove to Benson Street to Geogio Boutique. While the girls were looking at things, Kelvin slipped seven folded bills into the front pocket of Frank's Levi jeans. Frank pulled out the folded papers and counted eighteen bills in total.

They left Benson Street and went to LaMode Boutique on Broad Street. They made a final stop at Finger Gold Jewelry before going the Mama Sheriff Restaurant for its famous Ground Pea Soup. It was at Finger Gold Jewelry, that Frank slid a ring on Brenda's finger.

"Unite with me as one this second and always," he whispered.

Brenda felt her heart leap. It was her first time being so close to a boy. "Thank you," she said, looking at the ring, admiring it. "Frank, I hope it didn't cause you a fortune."

Caroline giggled, looking at Frank and Brenda. "I am sorry," she said, "but Frank is in love and doesn't count the cost."

"As it is said, 'the end will justify the means,'" Brenda said, smiling. "One attribute that will qualify you for this noble endeavor is patience and self-control."

On their way back to Paynesville, they dropped Brenda off by the gate to her house. Kelvin took off once she was inside her fence, and they continued their journey in silence.

"Who dropped you home," Brenda's mother asked her as soon as she entered the house. She stopped crocheting and put the needle and thread on the coffee table between the two sofas.

"Some friends," Brenda answered swiftly.

"Were they boys or girls," she asked further.

"Girls', Brenda lied.

"Don't disobey your father again," her mother reminded. "He told you not to get involved with people you don't know."

"They are former classmates who gave me a ride because getting a taxi from Town was hard," Brenda said. While speaking, the golden ring on her finger drew her mother's attention.

"I have never seen you with that ring before," her mother said.

Brenda's heart sank.

"Where did you get it from?"

Brenda extended her right hand without answering her mother, spreading her fingers. "This is my ring," she lied again.

"Go and change your clothes, so we can prepare something for your aunt."

# Chapter 14

"I am a lonely figure in the back seat," declared Frank.

"Yes! Brenda is no more with you," Caroline teased.

"I don't know if I will ever see her again," Frank said.

"You will if you are serious," Kelvin said.

"I am serious, Kelvin," Frank stressed.

"I know, but this generation of girls preferred to see you go after them like a skilled hunter," Kelvin said, sighing.

"Caroline tested me for almost six months before she could give in," Kelvin said. "Now I am the happier guy with this golden young chick. Right?" Kelvin said, turning to Caroline.

Caroline shrugged her shoulders.

They stopped at Caroline's Congo Town Residence, and everybody went inside. They met her mother at the dining table with a pile of papers before her. She was going through papers and running a line from top to bottom with her red pen, an English teacher at the University of Liberia.

She dropped her pen and asked, "How was the shopping?"

"Kelvin bought you a golden chain," Caroline said. "Let me put it around your neck."

Caroline put the chain around her mother's neck and closed the enclosure.

"It's so beautiful," her mother said, running her fingers along the chain. "Thank you, Kelvin."

"You are welcome," Kelvin said.

"Get something to eat, Kelvin, there's food."

"We are . . .," Kelvin said and stopped when Caroline quickly laid her pointer finger against his lips.

They sat and ate a little bit of the food. After eating, Kelvin and Frank thanked Mrs. Thomas and drove to Paynesville.

They drove in silence, as Frank had taken the passenger seat in the front. He was looking out the window. As they were crossing ELWA Junction, Kelvin asked, "Do you really love Brenda?"

"What?" Frank asked and adjusted his behind in the seat.

"I asked, do you really love Brenda?"

"Yes, Kelvin, I do. She's all I need now."

Kelvin could tell from the tone of his voice that he was indeed in love.

"We can arrange a time to visit her. But I hope it won't be like Hawa Cole."

"Kelvin, I'm sorry you felt terribly bad about the Hawa incident," Frank said. "Actually, I didn't love Hawa. Hawa's story was an outcome of a lustful thought."

"We will find Brenda . . . I promise," Kelvin assured him.

The rest of the ride was quiet until Kelvin dropped Frank and went home.

"How was the shopping," Kelvin's mother asked as soon as he entered the seating room.

His mother had a novel in her hand reading. She closed the book, placing her thumb to secure the page she was on. A bottle of Kontiki and a half-filled glass sat on the coffee table.

"Why the celebration," Kelvin asked.

"Your achievement," she replied.

Kelvin stopped and appeared confused. He went closer and sat by his mother. "Mama," Kelvin lowered his voice. He knew his mother and knew how to break through, especially when she took out a roadblock.

"Your father called to say you have gained admission to the University of Wales, UK. Son, I am so proud of you."

"Wow," Kelvin exclaimed. "Let me call my buddy to give him this info."

He hugged his mother and went over to the phone.

Frank hung up the phone and slugged into the cushion. He starred at the wall briefly, and back at the TV. It was commercial break, and Miata Fahnbulleh was advertising Liberian Crabs. The Liberian Crabs were exported to USA, Europe, and Asia, and the industry was booming but Miata was called in to boost it locally. Frank loves seeing lovely Miata in the water, mimicking someone buying Liberian Crabs and having them cooked for the family dinner. But the advertisement passed without Frank noticing Miata. His attention was on Kelvin and Ashmun; how each has secured a school to shape his future. His hope was still in the country's number one university, the University of Liberia.

University of Liberia (UL) was established as Liberia College in 1851. Liberia College went operational in 1862 and rebranded in 1951 as the University of Liberia. Par excellence in the eyes of the common people, UL was the light in the darkness that led Liberia's youthful population to the top, a duty to one's country. A champion against injustice and the touch for a new Liberia often referred to as *troublemakers* because of its military approach to making their voices (and those of the less fortunate) heard, UL was forced several times to close. An institution misunderstood and, most times, misjudged, UL was the only place available to pressure the government to deliver on its agenda. Students wrote pamphlets, spread leaflets, and even blocked public roads during their advocacy. Unfortunately, their voices did not match their performance. Most of the graduates who went into public service hoping to make a difference swam in the sea of sameness. Most citizens referred to UL as the house of flies, and students, upon graduation, turned to a whirlwind of hypocrisy. Such was Frank's only option for obtaining a higher education. Frank leaned sideways and pulled a notebook from his back pocket, flipped few pages and landed on his favorite quotes by the first President of Nigeria, Nnamdi Azikiwe, and read aloud: *There is plenty of room at the top because very few people care to travel beyond the average route. And so, most of us seem satisfied to remain within the confines of mediocrity.*

"Frank, you will succeed; it doesn't matter where you attend school. What matters is to be able to deliver with excellence and integrity what you have learned," he said to himself, slid the notebook back into his pocket and went to water the garden.

# Chapter 15

"Frank wake-up!"

At first it felt like a dream. Then it became louder.

"Frank wake-up man! Sleeping time like this," Kelvin's voice echo.

Frank rubbed his right hand over his face. "Kelvin," he voiced, drunk with sleep. "Why are you here so early?"

Kelvin sat on his bed and said, "My man, let's go and see Brenda."

"But...."

"My man, get ready," Kelvin insisted. "So, we can see the girl of your dreams."

"Really? Did you talk to her parents," Frank asked, sprung out of bed, and opened the back door to a mishit bathroom.

Pieces of broken tiles held by concrete made up the floor, and pieces of zinc held up by eight sticks planted into the ground shifted the bathroom into an oval shape. A passage-way is cast into the concrete to allow water to flow down the drain to the septic tank. The house had a modern bathroom restricted to the owner of the house.

Kelvin shrugged, nodding.

Frank's toothbrush between his teeth, toothpaste dropping onto the tiles, said, "What?"

Kelvin said nothing.

"Are you telling me we just walked into her yard this Saturday morning," Frank asked, spitting out toothpaste. Then he took in some water, switched it around in his mouth, and spat it out.

"It's not a crime in Liberia to just walk in someone's yard to say hello," Kelvin assured him. "Let's go, buddy."

Franks was convinced but had some hesitations.

"Scared," Kelvin asked.

"Me," Frank said with uncertainty. "I'm too grown for that."

"Then, let's go to see Brenda," Kelvin said.

"Wait," Frank halted him. "I have to tell my Papay first."

Frank walked to Mr. Rogers door; Kelvin tailed. He knocked and waited.

"Come in," came the voice.

Frank went into his father's room, and momentarily met up with Kelvin.

Kelvin parked a few feet away from the black Subaru parked closer to the balcony. They got down and went to the front door and rang the bell.

The Coopers were sitting in Livingroom watching TV. ELTV was rebroadcasting the Liberian Cultural Troop participation in EXPOs in South Korea and later, the USA. The competition had everyone fixated on the black and white TV. The bell rang for the second time.

"Brenda, get the door," her father said.

Brenda Scurried to the door and opened without asking who it was. She saw Kelvin and Frank and her heart dropped.

"My father's home," she greeted mouth.

"Really?" Franks replied and turned to leave.

Kelvin grabbed his wrist and pulled him closer. "We came to say hello to you," he said to Brenda.

"Brenda, who's at the door," Mr. Cooper called. "Let the person in."

Blood circulated with loud heartbeats and sweat oozed from her body. She stepped backward and held the door open for Kelvin and Frank. Kelvin immediately recognizes Mr. Cooper as he steps into the seating room.

"Mama, Papa, and Aunt Joyce, these are my friends, Kelvin and Frank," Brenda introduced her guests.

Brenda had never brought anyone to her house at eighteen and in a few months to turn nineteen. Her Aunt Joyce giggled. They exchanged greetings. Kelvin sat in the chair next to Brenda while Frank sat in the chair near the front door.

Mr. Cooper turned to Kelvin and said, "Young man, "have we met before?"

"Yes, Mr. Cooper," Kelvin replied quickly, "in my father's office."

Mr. Cooper stared at Kelvin, trying to figure out who his father was. "Who's your father?"

"Mr. David Benson, the National Bank governor," replied Kelvin.

Brenda was shocked. She didn't know that Kelvin was the son of the National Bank governor.

"Your father said you will be traveling to the United Kingdom for school," Mr. Cooper said.

"Yes, Sir," Kelvin replied.

"You are welcome to my home anytime," Mr. Cooper said.

Brenda took a deep breath and let it out quietly.

"Brenda, get some cornbread and beans; take your friends on the porch," her mother added.

"Kelvin, you never told me your father was the president of the National Bank," Brenda mumbled.

"I usually don't want my father's position to interfere with my life," Kelvin said. "I'm who I am. My father has built for himself a brand, and I am on my way to building mine. I don't want to build my life on my father's position."

After Frank and Kelvin sat, Brenda went inside the house. Her eyes met her aunt's eyes, and Brenda covered her heart with her right hand. Aunt Joyce smiled. Brenda grabbed a platter and placed two bottles of Club Mustitella and a bottle opener. Though the fear was wearing away, the impact was still visible. Brenda's hands were shaking as she placed a bottle on the table and struggled to open it. Kelvin eyed Frank. Frank got up and took the opener from Brenda, "I'll take it from here," he said.

Franked opened the bottles and placed the opener on the platter Brenda still had in her hands. She set the platter on the coffee table and sat on the third high back chair placed around the table.

"What brought you to my house," Brenda asked. "Did you guys miss me?" She turned to Kelvin and asked, "And where is Caroline?"

"She's home, but extended her greetings," Kelvin responded rather quickly. Then he turned to Frank and said, "My friend and brother, Frank, can't live without you."

"Is it because of Frank you came to see me?" she asked, looking at Frank from the corner of her eyes.

Frank nodded and smiled.

"You guys are lucky," she said and signed. "My parents welcomed you like you are Morris Dorley."

"Then, we must be special," Kelvin said. "Because Morris Dorley is a special gem, gifted to Liberia by the heavenly father."

"A gift that has not been recognizable by the system."

"The system has never recognized anyone who is nonpolitical," Brenda said. "Tecomsay Roberts, Fatu Gayflor, H. Wantue Major, James CoCo Chea, Caecar Gartor, T-kpan Nimely, Miatta Fahnbulleh, etc."

"Well," Frank said.

Everyone turned to him.

"Brenda, we came to ask you whether it's possible for you to be with us during the 26th and most of the holidays," Frank said.

"Sure," Brenda answered. "But I will have to get my parents' permission first."

"Ok, tell your parents we will get you on July 26th to go to the Jamboree at Caesar Beach."

"Frank is in love with you," Kelvin declared.

Brenda put her pointer to her lips to hush him. She didn't want her parents to hear the conversation.

"Do you want me to trust Frank," Brenda asked Kelvin.

Frank's eyes widened; he said, "I don't have anything to give as assurance, but my heart is fixated on you."

Brenda smiled and said, "I don't need your assets. Your heart is all I want. What is so important and delicate as your heart?"

"Nothing," Frank said. "My heart is my life and you have gained a place within its every beat. That's my pledge."

"Wow!" Kelvin exclaimed. "Oldman Gonda is with Garmai."

"Just like the Malawala Balawala movie," Frank added.

"Wait," Brenda raised her pointer finger. "This Garmai is different, not a trickster. But an honest Liberian woman who can give her heart without thinking about the consequences."

"Frank is a nice guy," Kelvin said.

Frank and Kelvin spent a few hours with Brenda at her parents' place. Since then, they have been picking up Brenda for social pleasures. But she was always home before her father's deadline of 9:00 P.M.

The affair between Brenda and Frank was concealed. Her parents' thought was Kelvin, the son of the National Bank governor, dating their daughter. Brenda would be seen with Kelvin, while Caroline would be with Frank at the Coopers' residence.

# Chapter 16

It was a foggy Christmas morning. As usual, it was as busy as all other Christmas mornings. The smell of food filled the air; dishes clicking in a rhythmic melody. Oldman beggars traveled through the streets and from house to house, accompanied by school children, dancing for pennies.

Brenda Cooper helped her mother prepare Christmas food in the kitchen. The Coopers decided to have collard greens and Rice during that Christmas. Brenda set the table and hurriedly took her bath. She had gotten her parents' approval and was awaiting Kelvin and others. They have planned to visit Hotel Africa that Christmas to watch the Malawala Balawala drama live on stage. Though they all planned on going to watch the show, Frank and Kelvin had their own plans.

Kelvin parked opposite the main entrance of the hotel. Caroline grabbed Kelvin's right hand and stood waiting for Frank and Brenda to disembark the vehicle. Brenda stepped out and walked over to Frank, smiling. He might have said something to her while they exited the car.

"Everything ok?" Kelvin asked.

"Yes, all is well," Frank said.

"Everything is good with you, right?" he asked Brenda.

"Yes," she answered quickly.

"Well, since everyone is doing good, I want to declare that this is the famous Hotel Africa. Whatsoever one sees here is a mirage. No need to rebroadcast it. So, this is it! Everyone on his own and God for all!" He said to Frank and Brenda, "We all meet here at 7:00 PM."

Frank set his watch to 6:45 PM.

Everyone rushed to the 4th Floor of the hotel. Kelvin and Caroline booked room 409, and Brenda and Frank booked room 412.

Frank went to the bathroom immediately when they entered Room 412. He bent over the face basin; being in a room with a girl, especially Brenda, the girl of his dreams, got his adrenaline going. He sprinkled some water on his face, but it didn't stop his heart from racing, and pumping enough blood into his body. It was his first time.

"No snacks?" she asked as she pulled and closed the drawers, one after the other. Frank rushed out of the bathroom after hearing the loud slamming of drawers.

"Hey," he held onto Brenda's shoulders. She was shaking like a hunted animal, staring at the floor. It was her first time to be alone with a boy in a room. A room many miles away from her secured home on 5Th Street, Sinkor.

"Look at me, Brenda," Frank said.

"Why?"

"I know you are scared," he said. "This is my first time too." Brenda at him.

"And you don't have to do anything you aren't comfortable about."

"What will Kelvin and Caroline think," she asked childishly.

"Let them think want they want to think," he said. "Let's sit down."

Brenda sat in the light gray accent chair at the far corner of the wall, and Frank sat on the bed.

"Right now," he continued, "I am happy you are with me, and we can talk all we want without interference."

"I saw locally bagged snacks in the hall," Brenda said. She opened her purse and pulled out a twenty-dollar bill. "Can you please get some for us?"

"Frank smiled and said, "Keep your money. Do you want polo, coconut or groundpea candies, or plantain chips?"

"Plantain Chips and Polo," Brenda answered.

Frank walked to the door, opened it, and allowed it to close behind him. In a second, the door opened again, and Frank came and slipped a piece of paper into Brenda's hand and dashed out of the room. Brenda stared, surprised. She opened the paper and written in bold letters was, 'Brenda, I love you like fish loves water'.

The note was extremely funny to Brenda. She erupted into laughter.

Frank went to the lobby, bought the snacks, and took the elevator to the fourth floor. He entered the room and found Brenda lying across the bed, sleeping like a baby. He was charmed by what he saw. A face untamed, pure, and fair, and a body not corroded by bleaching cream but polished by the good life and an excellent environment, producing a golden brownish skin covering an enviable body.

Frank quietly placed the items on the table, lay beside her, and fell asleep. His wristwatch alarm went off at 6:45 P.M. He jumped out of the hotel bed. To his amazement, Brenda was sitting at the table snacking.

"Was it you who wrote that statement," she asked him.

Frank sat up, rubbing his face. "Yes," he said. "I just wanted to make you laugh. I heard you laughing aloud from the elevator door."

"Thanks," Brenda said. "Frank, I love you like Firestone loves latex."

Frank smiled.

"It's time to go, my dear Brenda."

"Thank you, Frank," she said, smiling.

Frank extended his right hand, and Brenda placed her hand in it; they walked out laughing.

Since that time, Brenda and Frank had been meeting secretly.

# Chapter 17

Brenda got through reading a letter Frank had written and delivered through their contact. He was in Buchanan trying to get a job with LAMCO to earn some cash before the opening of the university. Though she had news to share with him, she awaited his return to Monrovia before telling him about it.

She walked into the kitchen with hands on her back like an overaged person. Mrs. Cooper turned and stared at her. The pink sweater Brenda was wearing swallowed both her hands and its length stopped at knee-high. It had been about three months since Frank and Kelvin visited her house.

Mrs. Cooper wrapped her hand around the mug, picked it up, and intermittently sipped it. Brenda greeted her, and she made an inaudible gesture. She walked by her mother and went to the kitchen. A piece of broken mirror was lying on the counter, exposing her image; a once desirable body was thin, exposing her collar bones; her lips, glowing and succulent, appeared like cracked clays; and her face took the form of a mature person. She quickly withdrew from the mirror and went to the cupboard.

Brenda pulled back her sweater sleeves and reached for a cup from the cupboard. She scooped spoonfuls of Ovaltine powder into the cup and added hot water. Then she pulled a stool closer and sat on it.

"Do you know Kelvin's home number," Mrs. Cooper asked Brenda. "I want to talk with him."

"About what, Mama?"

"I think it's time for both parents to talk about the relationship between the two of you."

"I don't know his home number," Brenda replied.

"Anyway, your father will reach Kelvin's father today to discuss you and Kelvin's future."

Brenda finished her drink, left the kitchen, and sneaked out of the house. She took a taxi to Paynesville to see Kelvin. The taxi got there just in time to see Kelvin driving out. She flagged him down and shared her mother's conversation with him.

"My father had asked me the same question and I told him the whole story," Kelvin said. "Get in."

Brenda took the front seat and fastened the seatbelt.

"Don't worry," Kelvin said. "I told my parents to play a low profile because I promised to handle it before traveling to the UK."

"I don't think my parents will accept Frank," Brenda said. "Why?"

Brenda said nothing.

"Why?" Kelvin asked again.

"Have you seen a 'country boy' marrying our kind?'

"What," Frank said incredulously.

"I thought we were all in the same boat, one nation, one people, and one Liberia."

"Why don't you tell your parents the truth," Kelvin asked.

"That's what I'm going to do," Brenda replied instantly.

"Well," Kelvin sighed. "Best of luck."

They drove the rest of the way in silence. Kelvin dropped Brenda at her gate and drove on.

"Kelvin brought you home," Mrs. Cooper greeted her daughter. "He will truly make a good husband."

"Really?" Brenda replied, found an empty chair, and sat.

"Yes," Mrs. Cooper replied. "Do you know what people will say about my daughter marrying the son of the National Bank," she said, raising raised both hands. "That's morale for this house."

"Mama," Brenda said, "I'm not in a relationship with Kelvin; it's his friend, Frank."

"What," Mrs. Cooper said incredulously. "Frank who?"

"Frank Dan."

"Dan," Mrs. Cooper said with disdain. "What kind of name is that? Will you be called Brenda Dan?"

Brenda sat quietly.

"Are you out of your mind!" Mrs. Cooper shouted. "Brenda, you have lowered the statue of this house!"

"Mama."

"Brenda, you better go to Kelvin and beg him for a switch."

Brenda stood up and said, "A switch? I'm not going to do that, Mama. He has his girlfriend, Caroline."

Mrs. Cooper shook her head, disagreeing.

"I can never do that," Brenda said.

"You must have a nice husband," Mrs. Cooper insisted. "Not a country rat. Certainly not a non-civilized son of a witch without a future!"

Mrs. Cooper walked closer to her daughter.

"Those people have no future in Liberia," she said. "And I don't know if they will ever have. You need to be ahead of your time, make decisions that will propel you into the echelon of powers and respect within Monrovia's social class."

Brenda scowled. "Can I go to my room, Mama," she said, hurried away, angry at her mother for calling Frank Dan a country rat.

"Yes . . . go to your room," Mrs. Cooper said, sighing. "Look at you and look at him . . . both of you together are incompatible! Do you want a husband that's a liability? What can he give you? What do you want? A husband that will cut palm for you?"

Brenda was out of hearing distance by then. She flopped into her bed with a heavy sigh. What's wrong with my mother? She's now one of the crossovers, she thought. She is of the Kru tribe, bearing the tribal name Yorkor, but took a western name, Mildred. A missionary family adopted her and sent her to school, and at the University of Liberia, she met my father, a settler lineage. During their senior year, they got married, Brenda thought, and thought, turning in bed. Her mother's statements haunted her. She hissed over and over.

"She has changed!" Brenda mumbled. "She is now *kwei*, replacing *country* rice with Uncle Ben's. She has deserted her people and looked down at them as poor, rejected, witches and wizards absorbed in superstitions and unbelief." Brenda sighed. "I admired my father," she continued. "He never looked at my mother as *Country* or *Congo* or *poor*, but as a beautiful Liberian woman who he chose to spend his life with."

Brenda heard footsteps approaching her room door. She waited, but it seemed the person changed direction and entered the next room.

All around the world, especially in the United States, enslaved Africans were forced to abandon their traditional customs and values and take on the cultures of the slaveholders. Most of the time, the enslaved will take on this new culture and advance it to another level. Like in Liberia, those of the native tribes who transitioned into the America-Liberia borrowed cultures saw themselves as above the people of their kind. They dropped their native languages, changed their names, refused to associate with the traditional customs and traditions, engaged in the exploitation of their people and country, well-schooled though but blinded by the false image displayed by Monrovia elites and the ruling oligarchy of tribalists, greedy, sycophants and, men and women around the presidency. It's mockery that 95% of the population of Liberia chose not to unite and distanced themselves from the reality that their people lived in riches. They refused to help educate their people and create awareness within villages of how to take control and tap into the vast resources at their disposal to transform these surpluses into rich Vai, Gola, Kissi, etc. communities. But they allowed their egoistic natures to help keep their people in poverty. They appeared (in the short term) better off than their fellow natives. A situation that encouraged envy, jealousy, witch-hunts, killing, witchery, fear, and further division amongst themselves.

The America-Liberians had within their mist those who wanted the natives to remain divided and poor. However, some opted for integration for a better Liberia.

After Bladen fled to Freetown, those who shared his views shattered into a splinter group. The Coopers remained in Monrovia, secretly indoctrinating natives and enrolling them in different schools. All of these are credited to John Cooper's second generation of the Coopers. John was a clerk for the

Division of the Interior. It aggrieved him so badly to see the Liberian Frontier forces carrying out the mandate of the government in Monrovia, by rounding up and flogging natives of the Kru tribes in Settra and Monrovia for the crimes of their kinsmen. A lot of them were hung.

At Liberia College, John completed a few courses taught by Bladen. He never became the same again. He and other students began to advocate for a Liberia for all, a contract to what the ruling establishment wanted. Though Bladen was in Freetown, he and his followers exchanged several notes requesting for a Liberia for all.

*"One can never leave the darkness of slavery in the United States and replicate that demonic and barbaric characters in Africa, on your brothers and sisters. Our freedom (that led us to travel to this great land of our forefathers) is not acquired to enslave our brethren in Africa but for us to liberate them through the gospel of our Lord and Savior, Jesus Christ...Our core plan is to see a Liberia for all,"* Bladen wrote.

John was devoted to the cause, and it became a rallying call for his family, a golden arch handed down to succeeding generations. Young Cooper entered Liberia College during the last year of Dr. J. Max Bond, Sr.

He automatically entered as a senior cadet of the Integration Movement at Liberia College, which was renamed the University of Liberia. An organization dedicated to fostering Edward Wilmot Bladen's called for the amalgamation of the natives and the Americo-Liberians to form a wholesome Liberia. The organization continued over the years and burned out like a candle, forming splinter groups that went into student politics and other religious and secular groupings after President Tubman announced his so-called Unification Policy.

Because Brenda's family had a long history of advocacy, she was sure that her father would understand and support her being with Frank.

# Chapter 18

It was around the Easter Holiday, and Frank was still in Buchanan, but he had been talking with Brenda on the phone, though not regularly. Brenda hadn't mentioned the pregnancy. Her father still had not been informed of it. Brenda believes her mother was still buying time for a Kelvin takeover. In the Cooper's residence, the name Frank Dan was never mentioned, only Kelvin Benson.

One quiet Easter Sunday afternoon, Brenda Cooper sat on the highchair around the kitchen island dining table sipping homemade lime juice. Her mother was baking cornbread for dinner with brown bean stew. Mrs. Cooper looked at her daughter and their eyes met. Mrs. Cooper smiled.

"I heard your cousin Jane, Aunty Pauline's daughter, got married to one of those top film stars in Hollywood," Mrs. Coopers said and turned toward the sink. She turned on the faucet.

"That's great," Brenda said.

"It's something about us," Mrs. Cooper said. "We marry good men, and Kelvin would make you a good husband. You just need to ask him to cover your shame."

Brenda simply stared at her mother. It has been four months, and her mother is still pressuring her to ask Kelvin to stand as the father of her pregnancy.

"Oh, Mammie," Brenda pleaded. "Can we have a conversation without bringing this up?"

Mrs. Cooper's adrenalin began pimping; her heart skipped a beat.

"Another thing!" Mrs. Cooper shouted and dried her hands on her apron. "Don't you know it's your future you are playing with?"

A vehicle drove into the yard as she was about to continue. She drew the curtains and saw Kelvin disembarking his BMW.

"Brenda, guess who is here?" she said, chuckling.

"Kelvin," Brenda said. "I know."

"Well, go and greet him."

"But Mammie, he knows where the door is."

"That is not a suitable way to encourage a man," Mrs. Cooper said.

"We aren't married, Mammie."

"So, what," Mrs. Cooper said. "He cares about you, you must reciprocate." Mrs. Cooper rested her hand on her daughter's right shoulder. "Baby Rose," she continued, "this is a man's world. Only those who play well will command the act."

The doorbell rang before she'd finished. Brenda hopped off the stool and ran to open the door.

"Hello, Kelvin," Brenda greeted. "Happy Easter!"

"I stopped seeing you," Kelvin responded. "I decided to come and visit. Sorry, I couldn't call earlier."

"You don't have to apologize, Kelvin," Brenda said.

"This is your home, too," Mrs. Cooper said, surprising everyone with her presence. "How are your parents? Come in and sit. I am baking some cornbread . . . you might enjoy some of it."

"Have you heard from Frank?" Brenda whispered as Kelvin made his way past Brenda and Mrs. Cooper.

"No, he's still in Buchanan. I was told he got a vacation job with LAMCO," Kelvin whispered. "I believe he is hustling for school."

"Kelvin, we must get out of here," Brenda mumbled. "Please, take me somewhere, for God's sake."

"We expected you yesterday," Mrs. Cooper said.

Kelvin felt flattered and sensed the direction of Mrs. Cooper's conversation. An idea occurred to him.

"Mrs. Cooper," Kelvin said. "Kindly allow me to take Brenda to the jamboree at Thinker's Village Beach."

"Yes, of course," Mrs. Cooper said, happily. "She's done helping with the household chores."

"I will be back," Brenda said and hurried to her room. "Is Caroline going with us?" she yelled from her room.

"Yes," Kelvin replied. "She's waiting for us in the car."

"Who is Caroline," Mrs. Cooper asked.

Brenda came out of her room and said, rather quickly, "One of our friends."

The sun was overhead, but its rays struck the brownish ocean sands exposing Liberia's late spring hot and humid climate. It was late April, a moderately hot month. The average temperature changes between 84.6 degrees Fahrenheit and 77.7 degrees Fahrenheit. But the recurrent ocean waves cooled the atmosphere. The Jamboree was organized to promote the launch of Tecumsay Roberts' MaSusu single. Though it showcases Teccumsay, big names in the Liberian music would perform. Those listed to perform on the program sheet were Miata Fahnbulleh, Morris Dorley, Zack and Gebah, Big Steve, Dave GQ, James Coco Chea including Princess Fatu Gayflor, Caesar Gartor, T. Kpan Nimely, Zaye Tete, Tokae Tomah, etc. A school of big-time Monrovia musicians is listed to entertain the audience to the break of dawn. However, Brenda Cooper had a curfew of 10:00 PM set by her parents.

T.Kpan Nimely sang his 'Fly was living before dog ear cut' when Kelvin, Caroline, and Brenda entered. The audience was doing a sing-along. The beach was jampacked; the trio had to struggle their way through the crowd. They landed on the third row from the front with Caroline standing between Kelvin and Brenda.

"I missed Frank," Brenda said.

Kelvin looked at her.

"Me too," Kelvin replied. "That boy loves the dancing business. If he was here, he would be partying."

Everybody laughed.

"Why can't you go to him," Caroline asked.

Brenda caught Caroline's eyes and smiled.

"If you truly love him, go to him," Caroline stressed.

"My parents . . .," Brenda said and stopped.

Her head hung and tears filled her eyes.

Caroline grabbed Brenda's hand and said to Kelvin, "Brenda and I are going to the ladies' room, please."

They struggled out of the crowd and headed to a rough cement block two-entry building. The lady's entrance was on the right, while the men were on the left. The entrance was crowded, and the girls had to wait for their term.

"Kelvin told me how your mother feels about Frank," Caroline said.

"Falling in love with Frank Dan is a crime that I have committed," Brenda said and sighed.

"Why?" Caroline asked. She could not comprehend the intent.

"He's a country boy," Brenda declared.

Caroline laughed and said, "Is that a crime?"

"I believe we can get in now," Brenda changed the subject and turned to the entrance.

"Does she know about the pregnancy?"

Brenda looked stunned. How does she know, she wondered.

"I knew the moment I saw you two months ago," Caroline said, smiling. "Kelvin's parents informed me about it. His mother even told me about what your mother suggested that Kelvin must tell your father that the pregnancy is his to cover up your shame."

Brenda could not believe what she was hearing.

"I think we should get back to Kelvin," Brenda suggested.

Her body began shaking as if she had instantly developed a nerve problem.

# Chapter 19

It was a joyous day in Liberia following the game between Liberia and Egypt. James Salinsa Debbah nailed the Pharaohs' one goal to nothing. Debbah is believed to come from Grand Bassa County. The lone goal created a discussion point for the county. People spoke the Bassa language throughout the Bassa country without fear of the embarrassment it created for strangers.

It was lunchtime; Frank Dan sat in the lunch hall eating a sandwich and listening to people speaking the Bassa language, which he couldn't understand. They talked as if he wasn't there. Frank remains there, feeling uncomfortable, but wishes he could understand what they were saying.

He was aware that he was from the northern portion of Liberia, a Gio or Mano boy, but didn't know which one and just couldn't understand or recognize any of his people's language. What is a man if you can't understand your language? That man is like a water without a source. Every family is gifted with these superior and unique different tonal ways to communicate, Frank thought. Yet, he felt cheated because he couldn't speak his people tongue nor distinguish Gio from Mano. He admired those who spoke their language, but dispatched those who yanked it from him.

Frank looked around; the other workers felt proud to associate Salinsa with the Bassa people. What will I say to my children, he thought. Will they continue their father's name without knowing what it means? Or will they be in the dark like their father, whose language is now replaced by this foreign language called English? A man without his original language is like a drowning man. Though he floats and sails away, hays of similar appearance ignite hope for survival. Frank knew that, so he clutched unto English like the Americo-Liberians. He gathered the spirits within him, reading all books, to master this foreign language, in speech and composition. Frank smiled as the discussion got louder and then faded as everyone disbursed into different departments.

Frank was fortunate to be employed in the workshop at the Washing Plant. A kinsman who knew his uncle got him the job. It had been three months since he was relocated to Yekepa, leaving Frank in Moore's Town, Bassa Community. Frank couldn't go with him because he had been admitted to the Wallenberg Training Center. It was then clear to Frank that his entry into the University of Liberia was never to be realized. He wrote to his benefactor expressing his gratitude for raising him. Frank also declared that it was time that he chose his own path. Therefore, he wanted to live in Buchanan where it was less competitive, the cost of living lower than Monrovia, and there were not many distractions. Kelvin and Ashmun, he believed, were out of the country, so he ruled out distraction. But Brenda is not a distraction, but an attraction. However, the real true is, he cannot live in Monrovia where two of his best friends were leaving for college and he sat waiting for the University of Liberia to open. It was rumored that the University of Liberia were looked at as the breeding ground for politicians, troublemakers, or political pundits. So, it was filled with spies, government operatives, and security personnel who were posted as students or faculties. Shutting down the university was just a matter of time. At the Washing Plant, it was quiet, and he was getting good at what he was doing.

Frank still had his sweetheart in Monrovia. It was six months since he last saw her. He had written to her twice and Kelvin once, but none had replied. "Well," Frank thought, "Out of sight out mind."

He rented a little room on the outskirts of Bassa Community near the Washing plant.

Frank was back in the Workshop, when he heard through the overhead speakers that the Boss wanted to see him. The boss was Henry Patterson, an American with an engineering degree from Virginia Tech. The Washing Plant was filled with lots of people from abroad; some could do their jobs, but others were just passing time for the salary. Kelvin passed four doors, and all were cut into departments headed by foreigners. They are the heads, paid big money and relaxed while the citizens do the dirty work and get paid less. An unholy alliance under the notorious Open-Door Policy between the foreign companies and the government of Liberia.

He remembered his friend, Ashmun, asking how wide he was; this opened the door and how long it had remained open. Frank agreed with Ashmun that this bad policy was and was never good for Liberia. Its true intention is to make a few rich, and many poor and benefit those who are willing to take the risk to spread a few dollars, bring in foreign-made goods, and suck all the nutrients out of the people and country while the government turns a blind eye. Ashmun and Kelvin believe these overnight investors will cut a deeper wound leading to an acute dependability that may take forever to heal.

So, as Frank headed to the boss's office, he became more curious. He only went to the boss's office once, which was the first day he was hired. He knew anyone who went to that office either came out happy or crying. All inquiring eyes were on him, as he knocked on the door.

"Come in," someone invited.

Frank pushed the door open and stepped in. His supervisor was seated at the mini-conference table. Their eyes met, and Frank quickly turned and looked at the boss, who told him to sit in an empty chair before his desk. The boss was seated behind his desk. Faint smoke traveled out of the cigar lying in the Marlboro cigarette holder.

"Frank Dan?" The boos asked.

"Yes, Sir," he answered, looking directly at the boss.

"Good job," the boss said, and extended his hand for a shake. "You have six months training at Wallenberg, Buchanan, and six months at Munich Technical University, Germany," he continued.

Frank's face lit up.

"Do you have a passport," the boss asked.

"No, Sir," Frank replied.

"Get one as soon as possible," he said. "And don't waste my time." The boss dismissed him with a wave of his hand.

Frank thanked the boss and his supervisor and walked out smiling.

"My Pekin," an older man in his department called out. "The receptionist was asking for you," he added.

Frank hurried to the entrance where the receptionist's desk was.

"You wanted to see me," he asked the lady sitting behind the desk.

She pointed at a boy seated opposite her desk in the visitor's area and said, "That boy is asking for you."

Frank recognized the boy, his next-door neighbor's son.

"Junior, what happened?"

"Someone came to the house, so Mama sent me to call you."

Who, Frank wondered.

"Uncle Frank," Junior said. "One fine woman . . . she fine ooo, Uncle."

Frank used his lunchtime to rush home. His home was about two minutes' walk from the Washing Plants. He and Junior walked to the house; questions about the mystery lady filled his head. His adrenaline started building up as he approached the house, and his heartbeat was uncontrollable. The sun was overhead; its rays heated up his anxiety-filled body, forming a chemical reaction soaking his faded dark t-shirt. His mind focused on Junior's parent Liberian Kitchen, where he anticipated the stranger was sitting.

Frank passed the house and walked to Junior's. He stood at the edge of the house, peeking into the kitchen. From his back, he heard a recognizable voice that sent an unexplainable shock as he struggled to process everything. Finally, he regained control and breathed out the name, Brenda Cooper.

"Brenda, what are you doing here," Frank said, incredulously.

"I came to see you, fool," Brenda replied.

"You came to see me?" Frank asked, childishly.

Some of the neighbors heard the interactions and came around.

"Frank stopped!" Brenda said. "I came to see. Stop all the drama." Brenda paused, took a deep breath, and let it out. "Now, where is your room? I want to take my bags inside."

"That's what I wanted to tell you," Frank cried.

Brenda felt embarrassed. "Frank," she said, grabbing his right hand and pulling him toward Junior's parent's house.

"No," Frank objected. "The other house is where my room is.

Frank led her to a rectangular-shaped mud building to a room with ten beds. This style of building is typical of Liberia, where the frames are made of sticks and bamboo, and the roof comprises round poles and aluminum zinc. What is unique about this style of building is the door to each room is directly opposite each other. When a door is opened, one will have a clear view of his neighbor's room.

Frank's room was the last room on the right. Brenda entered and saw a candlestand with a half-burnt candle stuck in it. Candlewax ran down and filled the stand, and drops of wax spread around the candlestand and onto the blue floormat. At the far end of the room was a mat the size of a yoga mat, and a little table with four technical and mechanical books.

"This is what I wanted to tell you," Frank said and sighed, collapsing into the only chair in the room.

Brenda smiled, and said, "Where do I sit?"

Frank got up and she sat.

"Please go and get my bags," she asked.

Frank left the room right away to get them. He returned with two suitcases, struggling with their weight.

"How did you get these things here," he said, incredulously, sitting the last one down.

"The taxi brought me here," Brenda replied.

He wondered how Brenda knew where to be dropped off.

"Frank, you can ask the question," Brenda said.

"Ok, Brenda, how did you find me?"

"I paid someone to find you in Buchanan, and they brought me to your house."

Frank laughed. "Brenda Cooper, you are not to be taken for granted," he said. "You are very much welcome here. I am only sorry you came to find me in these circumstances." Frank pointed out the condition of his room.

"Frank, I have never known you to be rich," she said. I didn't elevate my expectations."

Frank's eyes widened.

"I didn't think you had your own room by yourself," she said and smiled.

"So, you thought I was squatting on someone's couch?"

"Yes, why not," Brenda replied. "I brought money to rent a motel until I can get you a room."

She expected Frank to respond, knowing he wouldn't allow anyone to rain down words on him without a reply.

"Is that how lowly you think of me," he asked.

Frank moved to the other corner of the room. He stood, nervously rubbing his hair.

"No, Frank," Brenda said quickly. "I'm just kidding. I know you to be smarter than that."

Frank smiled. He returned to Brenda and sat on the floor, directly opposite her.

"How's your parents, Brenda," he asked.

"They are fine," she said. "I ran away from them."

"What? They didn't allow you to come?"

"Frank," Brenda said, "I just told you I ran away."

Brenda lifted her head and met Frank's eyes.

"Because I am pregnant . . . for you and I don't want them to suggest otherwise."

Frank Dan jumped to his feet. He paced around the room and returned to where she was sitting.

"What? Really?"

Frank thoughts ran through his mind, of reprisal from Brenda's family. He reminded himself of his status as a 'country boy.' He got on his knees at Brenda's feet.

"Please, Brenda, go back to your parents," he begged. "I'm afraid."

"Don't worry, they don't know where I am," Brenda said.

"I don't have anything to offer you right now, Brenda. I'm as poor as a church mouse."

"You said right now, right?"

"Yes."

"Ok . . . I plan on sticking around until you can care for me and the baby."

There was something in her voice that made her appear unbending. Frank felt she wasn't listening to him. He was scared, broke, and ashamed of the situation she met him in.

"Brenda," he said, "I am broke. Look at where I live . . . where I sleep is not fit for a pig. I can't take care of you. I love you, but I don't want you to leave the comfort of your parents' home for a place like this."

"I appreciate the sincerely," Brenda said. "That's what I was waiting for you to say to me."

Frank got up and walked to the window. He began pacing around the room, not saying anything.

"Are you going back to work," she asked.

"What time is it," he asked.

She looked at her watch.

"It's 12:47."

"I'm almost late," he said.

Frank grabbed his booth right out the room door and sat on the floor to put them on.

"I think you need a new pair of socks," Brenda suggested.

"What?"

"What time are you to be at work," she asked instead.

"At 1:30," he said and smiled. "Brenda, I am sorry."

"For what?"

"For not welcoming you appropriately," he said. "I sincerely appreciate you coming to find me. I never thought I would see you again."

"You acted like you were not happy to see me."

"I was afraid, Brenda; I don't want you to get in trouble with your parents because I will need their support in the future."

"Support?"

"If I am to marry you, I will need their consent," Frank clarified.

Brenda smiled. She knew her parents were frustrated and disappointed in her for leaving home without stating her location. But she was aware that Liberia was a small country; it didn't matter how long it would take to stay hiding; her parents would know her location. She hoped that she and Frank would have repaired the damage before they knew it.

"Brenda, today I was admitted to the Wallenberg Training for six months," Frank decided to share the news. "After the six months, I will travel to Germany for another six months."

"That's great!"

"Thanks," Frank said. "I believe you and the baby came into the good news," he said, smiling.

Brenda smiled.

"How's Kelvin," Frank asked.

"The last time I saw him, he was ok. I will tell you every-thing when you come back from work. You are getting late . . . did you eat?" she asked.

"No. But I am ok," he replied.

Brenda checked her handbag and pulled out a sandwich bag. It had two pieces of meat pie. She handed it to Franks.

"Thank you," he said and took them. Tears filled his eyes.

Since his uncle left for Nimba to spend the rest of his life in retirement, Frank had been struggling to make ends meet. Most of the time, during lunch, he hardly had anything to eat. A huge cup of cold water from the dispenser provides him the energy. But biweekly, he gave Junior's mother some money for food. He had discussed an arrangement with this single mother of six children, his neighbor.

Her husband died of an unknown sickness and was buried three months before Frank's arrival to the community. Her husband's grave was located right behind the house; fresh soil around it shows its newness.

This single mother woke up early in the morning and head-ed to Fanti Town to buy fish, which she sold at the 'Big Market' in Buchanan. If the business didn't go well, the leftover fish would be smoked, dried, and sold to buyers who prefer dried fish. Most of the time after work, Frank would have to wait for the lone meal late into the evening time, and everyone would eat at about 7:00 to 8 PM and go to bed. He would keep a little for the morning hours before going to work.

As it is said in Bassa, 'The one who keeps food until the morning hours is the person the children wait upon.'

Frank would warm his food (cold-bowl rice), and the chil-dren would surround him. He will have to share with them. If he doesn't have 'cold-bowl rice,' he will have to increase the quantity of water he intakes from the cooler, which he uses to refresh his dried and smelly mouth and stomach. Frank calls life in the community 'everyone on his own, God for all;' a Liberia saying projects poverty on all levels.

He appreciated that Brenda was there but was also scared of reprisal from her parents. When Brenda asked if he had eaten, he felt like crying because nobody had ever asked if he was hungry or if he was doing well. Frank stuffed the pies into his mouth like he had not eaten for many days.

It is often said that no knowledge is wasted. Brenda started as a data clerk with Index Logging Company, a company owned and operated by the Diggs Family of Monrovia. This company fell trees deep in the dense jungle of Moweh, Rivercess Territory, and shipped abroad. She worked her way up as a junior accountant for the company.

Frank had traveled to Germany and returned. LAMCO promoted him to junior staff and provided him with a home in Loop number one. Prior to Frank's return from Germany, Liberia was entering another phase of its existence; the disease of division that had long kept the country backward began to manifest. Those who visited the country in the past had mentioned this disease, but the Americo-Liberian hegemony had continually denied the presence of division. Yet, Edward Wilmot Bladen talked about it, the League of Nations investigated it (brought down President Charles D.B. King and Vice president), and it didn't change anything.

A new group emerged on the scene in 1973. The Movement for Justice in Africa was founded by Togba Nat Tipoteh and chartered in Ghana and the Gambia. Several similar groups sprung out, calling for the redistribution and equity of land, wealth, and political leadership.

Brenda gave birth to a baby boy at the LAMCO hospital, and Frank named him Gonda Gerald Dan. A few days later, she was taken home.

On the 1st of December, a Friday, Matilda Newport Day, a holiday in Liberia, a navy-blue BMW stopped in front of the Dans' residence in Loop One. The LAMCO residential community was called the loop, the extension of the company's operation in Buchanan, Grand Bassa County, near the Atlantic Ocean. LAMCO mined the ores about 251 kilometers in the north, Nimba County. The company built and operated rails that were used to transport the mined ores from the Nimba plant to the Washing Plant in Buchanan, where it was processed or washed before being shipped abroad. LAMCO also used the rail to transport passengers to and from Nimba to Buchanan. It eased the long drive from Monrovia to Yekepa, Nimba County. A gem that the future government will abundant and increase the suffering of getting to Nimba through the motor road.

Brenda heard a car driving through the crushed rocks spread through the driveway and wondered who the early visitor at their doors would be. She was singing to her baby while preparing his food. Fixated on the sound drawing closer to her door, the kittle whistled startling her. Brenda turned the stove off and pulled back the curtain to see who it was that had stopped in her yard.

Frank was still in bed; he worked until 4:00 AM that evening. Brenda's heart sank below when four figures emerged out of the vehicle. She immediately recognized two of the four and hurried to the room leaving the baby in the living room. He was in the cradle kicking his feet into the air while his mother was preparing his food.

"Frank," she said and taped his chest. "Wake up, my parents are here."

Frank sprung out of bed. "What do we do now? "Pretend like we not home?"

"Our cars are out there," she said. "They will definitely know we are hiding."

"How did they know we live here," Frank asked.

"I have no idea," Brenda replied.

"We cannot keep running," Frank said.

Brenda stared at him, showing a weak smile. "There are four persons all together," she said.

"Four persons," Frank said incredulously and jumped out of bed.

"I think I saw four persons," Brenda concluded.

Suddenly the doorbell rang, and the baby began crying.

"We knew this day would come," Brenda said, tapping Frank's shoulders. "Let's face it and fix it once and for all."

"Get the door while I put on my shirt," he said.

Brenda headed to answer the doorbell but stopped in the bedroom doorway. She turned and looked at him, and he remembered the familiar expression on her face.

"Any plan," he asked.

"Let's tell them how sorry we are . . . as soon as they entered."

"Brenda," he whispered, "we hurt them."

"Yes," she replied. 'That's why we're sorry."

The doorbell rang again.

"Get dressed and follow me," Brenda suggested. "Do as I do, ok?"

Frank nodded.

He put on a T-shirt and followed her to the sitting room. Brenda went to get the door while Frank tried consoling the crying baby.

"Mama . . . Daddy," she greeted, getting on one knee as soon as she opened the door. "We are so sorry for everything."

"Excuse me," Mrs. Cooper said. "I want to see my grandchild."

Her mother rushed by her and went to the baby right away. Frank handed the baby to Mrs. Cooper.

"Kelvin . . . Ashmun . . . ,' Frank exclaimed when he saw the rest of the visitors walk in. "You came along with Mr. and Mrs. Cooper?"

They were following behind Mr. Cooper. Frank greeted Mr. Cooper and then hugged his friends. Brenda was still frozen on her knee; her father extended his hand, and she took it.

"Papa," she said, as tears filled her beautiful eyes.

Mr. Cooper said, "Come and give Daddy a hug."

She got up and threw her arms around him. Their hug trickled memories which came back with a fresh gentleness and tears. Brenda remembered she had always come home from school running into those arms.

"I am sorry, Papa," she whispered.

"It's okay . . . it's ok. I always knew where you were and how you were doing."

"Really?"

"Yes," Mr. Cooper said. "Your employer, Mr. Diggs, is a cousin of ours . . . third cousin from your grandmother's lineage. He told me about all your progress."

Brenda then realized that the promotion was not her making but a family connection. Her father read her face correctly.

"He also told me about your promotion and how you are a smart and hard worker. I am proud of you."

"I thought you were angry with me for leaving," Brenda said.

Their embrace ended, and Brenda said, "Hello, Kelvin. Hello, Ashmun . . . thanks for coming. I was so happy to see my parents that I forgot to greet you."

"You were afraid," Kelvin joked in a whisper.

She smiled.

"What is his name?" Mrs. Cooper asked.

"Gerald," Brenda said.

"Gonda," Frank added.

"Okay. I will stick with Gerald," Mrs. Cooper said. "He looks more like his grandmother."

Everybody turned to Mrs. Cooper.

"You are his grandmother," Frank said, smiling. "Who else will this child resemble?"

'So, there is no resemblance of his father or his father's parents?' Frank thought to himself. "We were once kings, the Dans."

He remembered his uncle's words echoing loudly into his head. This is exactly what the Republic of Liberia wanted: destroying everything 'kingly' that belongs to us. Allowing us to exist like a snake whose head had been cut off. They knew our strength was our loyalty to our kings and individual communities.

Frank's eyes were fixated on Kelvin. He was speaking but his words were inaudible. Frank observed that the Republic of Liberia could not take both from the natives. So, they destroyed all connections of loyalty to the kings, replacing it with commissioners and chiefs' systems and leaving loyalty to individual communities. To this day, Liberians pay homage to counties and tribes than to the Republic of Liberia.

"Frank . . . Frank, are you listening to me," Kelvin asked.

"What were you saying," Frank asked.

"We need to talk to you," Ashmun said.

"Mr. Cooper had increased the volume of the TV.

"I think we need to go somewhere quiet," Kelvin suggested.

Frank suggested they go outside and stand by the car. They did.

Benda joined her mother.

"Mama, we need to talk," she said.

Mrs. Cooper, still holding the baby, followed Brenda to the veranda.

"This boy brought Cooper's friskiness," Mrs. Cooper joked.

She sat down with the baby and Brenda sat on the opposite chair.

"Mama," Brenda said. "I am so sorry for the pain I caused you and Daddy."

Brenda tried so hard to avoid eye contact with her mother. She lowered her head but peeped once or twice to watch her mother. In the meantime, the three friends gathered next to the car to converse.

"I sued the Republic of Liberia; did you hear about it?" Ashmun stated.

"Really," Frank asked. "What for?"

"For denying the right to operate my business as a citizen of the Republic of Liberia."

"But the constitution said so," Frank said.

"Yes," Ashmun agreed. "The constitution is racist. We need a referendum that will alter this stupidity."

"The foreigners will take over this land." Kelvin snapped.

"Kelvin, who are the foreigners," Frank asked.

"The Lebanese, Indians, and other foreigners," Kelvin answered.

Frank was not satisfied with his answer. "Really," he asked. "Most of those Lebanese, Indians, and others who are in this country were born here. Their forefathers are dead and gone. Are they not Liberians?"

"Most don't know any other country other than Liberia," Kelvin said. "They are Liberians . . . we need a referendum. People know but the leader preferred to bury their head in the sand."

"You see, this is why we must change the laws," Ashmun said. "Why would you deny me citizenship when you honored my father's father with a street? And you see, the rejected children are the richest in this country."

"Wait," Frank said, raising both hands. "Was old man Monie Captan a citizen of Liberia when he became Foreigner Minister?"

"I don't know, but he served," Ashmun responded.

"That's hypocrisy," Frank said. "Citizenship should not be on a 'pick-and-choose' basis."

"But who then is a citizen and who is not a citizen," Kelvin asked.

"This is why we need to take power," Ashmun said. "To change the status code."

"I believe that we can only arrive at a peaceful and prosperous Liberia when we cling to our diversity," Kelvin said. "Though it a hard and bumpy road, we stand united."

"How do we take power," Frank asked.

"By forming a political party," Ashmun replied. "You be our political leader."

"Me," Frank said incredulously. "I cannot speak Gio or Mano."

"It doesn't matter; your last name matters," Kelvin injected. "According to history, the Dans are known throughout the land before Liberia was established."

"Can I have a minute," Frank asked.

He walked about five feet away from Kelvin and Ashmun.

'This is my country, and my children's future depends on what I do about or with this country,' he thought. 'If God endowed me with a long life and if I start to die in my late forties, Liberia will forever remain my home.

He lifted his head, saw Brenda and her mother in a warm embrace, and smiled, knowing Brenda, for her smartness and her know-how to restore peace, would make a great first lady. But what kind of president would I want to be? He asked himself over and over. A president for the Christians (although I am a Christian) A president for the Gios and Manos? A president who will pay back the Americo-Liberians for what they did to my generation. Or a president whose only wish is to fill the pockets of my crony and me? Or will I be a president who will watch his people suffer and continue to live in abject poverty without doing anything to better their lives? Since I will be the president of Liberia, I will be the president for all, and their well-being is my responsibility.'

His friends watched him to where Brenda and Mrs. Coooper were, then he took Brenda to one side, and they talked for a good moment before returning to them.

"The first thing a good president would do is keep his house in order," he said. "I will have to marry Brenda Cooper."

"That we know," they responded in chorus, smiling.

"I accept," Frank said, "but who will be my vice?"

He looked at Kelvin.

"Ashmun," Kelvin said, pointing.

"Ashmun," Frank said incredulously.

"Why not," Kelvin asked.

"Ashmun is too white to be my VP," Frank objected.

"You sound like a typical old-school Liberian," Ashmun said. "If we need to change the status code and provide hope, we must do the unthinkable."

"Like advocating for the restoration of the kingship system that will connect the missing link," Frank declared. "Restoring all tribal land to the authority of each tribal king. A move that will restore tribal authority to one that will (to be elected by each tribal kingdom), be a protector of this people's land and values and a person or group of people on a counsel, subjected to the laws of Liberia . . . a system that corrects the wrong like my case, having royal blood but living like a slave. Lifting me is what hope is; making Liberia the breadbasket of West Africa is the true demonstration of hope and purpose."

The friends listened.

"Like allowing all kids (black or white) born in Liberia, citizens," Frank continued. "That's what hope is . . . hope is not calling one group of people names and trusting non-Liberians over Liberians. Jealously protecting all Liberian Businesses; proposing a Liberian first policy throughout the length and breadth of Liberia."

"Like revisiting all lands in and around the country . . . the lands that had been undeveloped for more than ten years be put in the spotlights," he went on.

"Like rezoning all the land in the country, developing a numeration system for each house, and digitalizing Liberia, celebrating November 29th Liberian Day (A Day set aside for all to demonstrate their Liberianess, etc. And above all else, use love to heal the wound of our past," Frank added and raised his fist.

Kelvin and Ashmun raised theirs too. They connected their fists to Frank's. They shouted in unison, "For a diversified but united Liberia,"

"Liberia, a country established by freed negroes and white agents from the United States," Ashmun declared. "A land whose history is incomplete without the history of black people in the United States. A place is unfinished if the history of the struggles of the natives of the Green Coast is not rewritten to be internalized . . . the only place that has a direct link to all African Americans in the United States and a place they can call home."

"And all other places outside of Liberia that are championing a haven for black people in the United States is a faux pas," Kelvin added. "If a country is marketing colonial master depository as the beginning of the evil and strenuous journey of a slave to the new world, it's falsehood. The journey of a slave from the interiors to the local holdings, to the boats or ships to be taken to the Senegal or Gold Coast then to the new world."

"Gentlemen," Frank said, "the history is there. Now let's think about giving our people hope and self-determination . . . let's join Morris Dorley and sing: *Mama oo, Liberia is my home!*"

"*Anywhere you will go . . ..*" Kelvin sang.

"*Liberia is my home,*" Brenda joined the friends' singing.

# *About the Author*

Shedrick Bricks Seton Sr was born in Harbel, Firestone Plantation, Liberia. He attended Bassa Demonstration School, and later, Firestone School System. Mr. Seton attended the Assemblies of God Mission High School in Sinkor before graduating from the University of Liberia, earning a BA in Political Science.

Seton began writing short stories in the eighth grade at Firestone School System. After graduating high school, he continued composing for FunTime Magazine in Monrovia and later for CandleLight Magazine and Pleasure Paper. Fate of the Unknown is this third novel. He has authored two novels: The Falcon (2016) and Forget Me Not My Love (2020).

Mr. Seton is a member of the YMCA of Liberia and the President's Young Professional Program (PYPP). He is married to Anita Siah Anderson Seton, and they have four children. Mr. Seton lives with his family in Fredericksburg, Virginia, USA.

# Books by Shedrick B. Seton

*AVALIBLE EVERYWHERE BOOKS ARE SOLD*
*paperback and ebook*

# Connect with Author

Readers of this book are encouraged to contact
Mr. Shedrick B. Seton with comments:
*Email: shanitakseton@gmail.com*

Visit author's Facebook page:
*https://www.facebook.com/shanitakseton*

Village Tales Publishing provides traditional publishing services and turnkey services to individuals that seek to successfully self-publish and promote their books. We handle all aspects of publishing; editing, cover design, production, marketing and order fulfillment.

Please visit our websites:
www.villagetalespublishing.com
www.oass.villagetalespublishing.com

Join our mailing list for updates on new releases, deals, bonus content, and other great books from Village Tales Publishing.

Email Us:
villagetalespub@gmail.com

****

Like Us on Facebook
www.facebook.com/villagetalespublishing
Follow Us @villagetalespu

www.ingramcontent.com/pod-product-compliance
Lightning Source LLC
Chambersburg PA
CBHW070523260626
47161CB00004B/1627